COMPROMISED IDENTITY

JODIE BAILEY

D0011015

◆ HARLEQUIN® LOVE INSPIRED® SUSPENSE

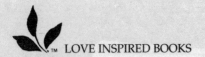 LOVE INSPIRED BOOKS

Recycling programs
for this product may
not exist in your area.

ISBN-13: 978-0-373-44716-9

Compromised Identity

Copyright © 2016 by Jodie Bailey

www.Harlequin.com

Printed in U.S.A.

"Are you always this prepared?" Jessica asked.

Her voice sounded laced with skepticism and not a trace of fear. She tended to stay calm in the moment, he'd already seen, but he also knew she'd been close to tears at some point.

"Only when I've already had to save an asset's life three times."

Jessica peeked around him at the man lying trussed on her bathroom floor. Her head tilted, expression darkening. "That's the man who was hiding in my car."

Sean gave a slight nod, watching her. She was afraid, he could see it on her face, but she wasn't about to give in and weaken in front of him.

Most likely, she didn't want him to see she was terrified. That was nothing to be ashamed of. Three attempts on her life in two days would rattle even the most battle-worn vet, especially on home soil where it was supposed to be safe.

For the first time in a very long time, Sean felt the urge to pull a woman close and comfort her. But no matter what he felt, distance was necessary if he was going to put his life and his career back together.

Jodie Bailey writes novels about freedom and the heroes who fight for it. Her novel *Crossfire* won a 2015 RT Reviewers' Choice Best Love Inspired Suspense Book Award. She is convinced a camping trip to the beach with her family, a good cup of coffee and a great book can cure all ills. Jodie lives in North Carolina with her husband, her daughter and two dogs.

Books by Jodie Bailey

Love Inspired Suspense

Freefall
Crossfire
Smokescreen
Compromised Identity

The thief cometh not, but for to steal, and to kill,
and to destroy: I am come that they might have life,
and that they might have it more abundantly.
–John 10:10

To the men and women of the US military, who fight battles
within and without so that we can know peace.
And to their families, who bear their warriors' armor
and fight right beside them.

ONE

"I'll gather the Casualty Notification Team."

Staff Sergeant Jessica Dylan twirled her pen on the green cloth cover of her notebook, watching the black barrel spin to stop, pointing straight at the chaplain, who'd stood to gather his papers after leading the casualty briefing for rear detachment. She couldn't shake the thought of a family who was going about their business right now, thinking everything was right in their world.

"You okay?" Captain Alexander, the battalion rear detachment commander, stopped behind her on his way out the door. "Did you know Specialist Murphy?"

"Only by sight."

The captain didn't even hear her. He'd already moved on, out the door before her reply could even get to him.

Jessica stacked her things and pushed her chair back, feeling older than her twenty-eight years. This was no way to start a Monday.

No, she hadn't known Specialist Murphy, but she could picture his mischievous grin at the Family Readiness Group picnic when he'd paid half a week's pay to shove a cream pie in his First Sergeant's face. It was true to form for Murphy. He'd taken every opportunity to buck his chain of command. Having license to do it publicly, even for a fund-raiser, had apparently been too much for him to resist.

Pulling the book tighter against her chest, Jessica shook off weighted emotion as she walked across the small courtyard from headquarters to her company's building. Death never got easier. If the captain wasn't going to get upset, neither was she. She could fall apart when she got home away from anyone who would see her grief as a weakness.

Her boots thudded heavy on the industrial tile, but they slid to a stop as she neared her office. The door was cracked slightly, light from her huge windows leaking into the dark hallway.

She shoved her hand into her uniform pocket, feeling for the key, vividly remembering how the lock had stuck as she'd left for the casualty briefing. With her Rear D soldiers on a detail across post and everyone else of consequence in the briefing, there was no one who should have needed access to her office.

Laying her book on a desk in the outer office, she peeked around the corner.

A female soldier, her back toward the door, stuffed Jessica's work laptop into a small black backpack, but her focus stayed on the desktop's screen. She fidgeted back and forth as if she was waiting for something, then reached under the desk, pulled something from the computer's tower and shut the machine down, just like Jessica had left it.

It had only been a couple of weeks since her other laptop was stolen, and that theft had brought wrath down on her head. No way was she going through that again. Jessica stepped back, giving the woman just enough room to exit the office. Arms crossed over her chest, she waited.

The door pulled fully open, and Specialist Lindsay

Channing stepped out, intent on shutting the door quietly behind her before she turned. When she spotted Jessica, her steps stuttered backward. "Staff Sergeant Dylan. I didn't expect to see you here."

"Funny." Jessica dropped her arms and balled her fists loosely at her sides. "I could say the same thing about you. Care to explain?"

Channing's gaze darted from Jessica to a spot up the short hallway, then to the floor before going back to Jessica. "I was just coming back from a meeting and was going to stop by and give you some paperwork but your door was open and…" She took a step forward, sliding the backpack into her hand.

"Try again."

"That's the truth." Channing smiled slightly and then edged to one side, trying to slip around Jessica.

Not on her life. Not until she coughed up what she'd been doing in that office. Jessica stepped sideways with her as Channing lashed out and swung with the heavy backpack, catching Jessica against the temple.

Something clattered to the floor as the blow drove Jessica to the right and slammed her shoulder into the cinder block wall, shooting pain through her body like electricity. It took a moment for the world to clear, and Channing was running up the hall for the exit.

Jessica tried to shake off the blow, doubling over with her hands on her knees, shoulder screaming from contact with the wall. A few feet away, what had to be Specialist Channing's cell phone glinted in the sunlight. Jessica shoved it in her leg pocket and took off out the door in pursuit, though each fall of her boots on the floor jarred an unbearable pounding through her.

One of the young soldiers on staff duty, tasked with keeping watch over the battalion area, stepped out of the headquarters building as Specialist Channing raced across the courtyard, flinging the backpack into the bushes as she ran.

"Call 911!" Jessica shouted at him as she rushed past, pushing to gain on the thief, praying he'd follow the order instead of gawking at their backs.

Jessica's world spun in the chill of a November Kentucky afternoon, the ache in her shoulder intensifying in the cold. She would not let this slow her down. She. Would. Not. Rounding the corner of the building at the parking lot, she stopped and grabbed the rough metal of a small fence, willing the pain to stop, watching as a small red sports car screeched into the parking lot, throwing gravel in its wake.

Channing dove into the passenger's seat, but the car didn't move.

Gathering her reserves, Jessica pushed away from the fence and stepped forward, prepared to confront anyone who tried to get in her way. She was not going to get called on the carpet for another missing laptop. Her career couldn't take that blow.

A man in civilian clothes climbed from the car, reaching into his coat for something she couldn't see, setting off alarms that refused to be silenced. His dark eyes raked across her as he paused beside the vehicle not twenty yards away.

Jessica took a step back, catching her foot against the fence, reaching out to brace herself as the man pulled his hand from inside his coat, a thick knife glinting in the late-afternoon sun.

Staff Sergeant Sean Turner was out of his small rental car and halfway to the building when the man exited the little red sports car and stalked toward Staff Sergeant

Dylan. Three days he'd been pulling surveillance on her and nothing. Now, everything exploded at once.

He pushed hard across the asphalt as the man pulled a knife and stepped closer to his victim.

If Jessica Dylan died in front of him, Sean would have one more sin to add to his list of unforgivables. That list was long enough already. "Back away!" The shout echoed off the buildings on the other side of the nearly deserted parking lot, competing with his footfalls for volume.

The man straightened and whipped around, knife at the ready.

This was not going to be fun.

Especially not without his weapon and with his shoulder still healing. There was no way to get authorization to carry a gun on post without compromising the mission. He'd have to get through this altercation with what existed inside his own skin.

Holding up his hands to show he wasn't armed, Sean stopped a few feet away from Jessica Dylan, edging slowly to the left to put himself between the man and his prey. "If you put down the knife, we'll stop this now." He motioned for Jessica to slip around the end of the fence—anything to put a barrier between her and the man creeping closer.

"Staff duty called the police." Jessica spoke from behind him. "They should be here any second." There was no fear in her voice, just fact.

If the situation weren't so dire, Sean would break away to high-five her cool in the heat of battle. She didn't even sound out of breath.

The other man didn't flinch at Jessica's declaration. He took a step to the left, seeming to calculate the shortest distance around Sean to Jessica. Never once did he turn back toward the car, his likely escape route.

Sean's heart hammered harder. Whoever this guy was, his focus wasn't on getting away. It was squarely on Jessica Dylan.

That changed everything. If keeping her quiet was more important than saving his own life, there was more at stake here than it seemed on the surface. This guy had to have orders from someone who scared him more than jail time.

Sean balled his fists and stepped forward, leading the offense rather than playing defense.

"I wouldn't do that," a second voice called out from the red sports car.

The female soldier who had run from the building stood by the passenger door, pistol aimed over the roof at Sean.

Nope. Not fun at all.

The back of Sean's mind tried to spin up images of the last time he'd been unarmed and cornered, of the nightmarish days that followed, but he swallowed the fear and refused to give in. That was last time. This time, he had to win. His life wasn't the only one to consider.

And he had orders of his own.

Sirens spun up in the near distance, stealing the two assailants' attention for the brief second Sean needed. "Run!" He fired the word over his shoulder to Jessica, hoping she'd obey.

Her attacker was already in motion, diving through the door of the car before Sean could even get traction to follow him. As soon as his accomplice was inside, he floored the vehicle in a spray of gravel as the scene exploded, a military police cruiser roaring into the parking lot as two more soldiers ran around the corner of the building.

Sean waved an arm toward the sports car and yelled to the police. "That's them! Go!" The car hesitated, and then took off in pursuit. Satisfied the officers had things in hand, Sean turned his attention to the woman he was supposed to be keeping an eye on.

Jessica Dylan sagged against the chain-link fence, fingers laced through the metal as she watched the car roar away. The instant she realized he was watching, she straightened and tugged the hem of her jacket, her face rearranged into an impassive mask.

This was a soldier who wanted him to know she was fully in control. No victim here.

Before he could reach her, the two soldiers who'd raced from the building swarmed her, but Staff Sergeant Dylan waved them off. "I'm fine." She turned on two of the younger soldiers, eyeing them with an expression Sean hoped he never saw aimed in his direction. "Explain to me how Specialist Channing got into the company building when it was locked."

Must be staff duty. And one of them had made a huge mistake. For their twenty-four-hour shift, those guys were responsible for manning the area and making sure everything stayed safe and low-key. From walking the battalion to answering the phones, they were the first line of defense. Sean would like to know the answer to how this all went down right in front of them, as well.

One of the soldiers stepped forward and Sean angled to read his name. Specialist Thompson. "I had stepped away to take a message to Captain Alexander. My runner was at the desk."

Staff Sergeant Dylan tipped her head toward the younger soldier, a Private Meyers. "So you let her in?"

"She needed to drop something off in your office, so I let her in and came back to my post. I didn't think it was a big deal." Private Meyers kept his gaze just over Jessica's shoulder.

Sean couldn't blame the kid for not looking at her. He was facing a world of hurt leaving the desk unmanned and giving access to a soldier on the very day trouble went down. Sean stepped closer, drawing Staff Sergeant Dylan's attention again, and she stepped away from the other soldiers to approach him, left hand extended, the only indication she'd been through trauma: a slight tremor in her fingers.

"I'm Staff Sergeant Jessica Dylan." She grasped his fingers tightly in hers, her hand chilled from the elements and likely mild shock. "Thanks for stepping in."

Something was wrong. Sean released her hand and eyed her carefully. "Most people I know extend their right hands, Staff Sergeant. Are you injured?" The way she angled her shoulder slightly back was a telltale sign. He looked past her to the two soldiers trudging back toward their post. "Private Meyers, call for an ambulance."

"Meyers." Jessica Dylan pulled herself taller and turned her back to Sean. "Do not. I'm fine."

Meyers and the other soldier hesitated, and then seemed to choose their own chain of command over the random stranger, turning to walk back toward the building. Only Private Meyers cast an uncertain, slightly amused glance back at them.

She whirled on him so fast she wavered on her feet. "I don't know who you are, but I said I'm fine." Her eyes swept the rank on his chest, and she seemed a little prideful to find it equal to hers: Staff Sergeant.

Holding his hands up in surrender, Sean took a step

back, giving her space before she took out her anger and fear on him.

"I'm fine, by the way. Just took a dive into the wall shoulder first. I'll have it checked out, and I'm sure it will be bruised tomorrow but none the worse for wear." She met his eyes with authority. "Again, thank you. I don't know what made you do it, but I appreciate the help." Without looking back, she turned and walked away.

The help? He took two steps to follow her, then stopped, unsure whether he should reveal his mission yet or not. Based on all he'd seen in the past five minutes, that man would have killed her. Without Sean, Jessica Dylan would be dead.

TWO

Shoulder throbbing with a very new and totally unwelcome kind of pain, Jessica sank to the wooden bench by the side door in her house and bent to unlace her boots, wishing the pain meds would kick in and give her relief.

"At least the doctor said nothing's broken." Her roommate, Angie Hunter, slipped off her shoes and kicked them under the bench.

Jessica had to dodge to keep her ankle from being pierced by heels so tall that airport security would likely consider them weapons. "At this point, I think I'm past caring." She'd toughed it out in front of everybody, not wanting to get carted off in an ambulance like a weak female, but the pain had finally driven her to make sure the injury wasn't more than it seemed. All she needed was a pointless injury to sideline her career. The doctor at the emergency room had assured her nothing was torn or broken, but he had told her to take it easy for a few days. Hopefully, his prognosis on how long the pain would last was wrong.

Stowing her boots under the bench, Jessica followed Angie into the small kitchen at the back of the house, letting a deep breath of the familiar spicy scents wash over her and ease some of the weirdness from her day. This room, with its cheery yellow walls and white cabinets, was her happy place, the one spot in the whole world where nothing could touch her. Running her hands along the cool granite of the counter, she thanked God again for leading her to a roommate who had gourmet decorating tastes, if not gourmet cooking skills.

"Hungry?" Angie pulled open a cabinet door and stood staring into the contents as though she knew what to do with them.

"You're cooking? I'll pass." Jessica leaned back against the counter. No matter who was cooking, food didn't sound appetizing with the pain in her shoulder twisting a knot in her stomach. Or maybe that knot had more to do with the fact Channing and her cohort were still out there somewhere, having eluded the MPs and slipped off post before the order came through to tighten security at the gates.

"I make a mean can of tomato soup, I'll have you know." Thumping the can on the counter, Angie reached up and pulled her blond hair into a ponytail, securing it with a hair band she slid from her wrist. "You should eat something."

"I'm good. All I want is a shower and my bed."

"Maybe you'll dream about your mystery protector." Two years younger than Jessica, Angie thought everything was romantic. Knowing her, she was wishing she had been the one facing down a bad guy while a handsome hero rushed to save her.

Reality was nothing like the fantasy. Jessica would roll her eyes, but she was afraid she'd fall asleep halfway through. "I'm good. Thanks."

"Just tell me he was cute, and I'll go dream about him for you."

"I was a little too busy to notice." Sort of. In spite of

the situation, forgetting how blue those eyes were when he trained them right on her was not easy. And he had that dark blond kind of hair that was just a little bit longer than it should be, so it sort of mussed on the top as if he'd dragged his fingers through it.

Well, okay. So a girl could think a guy was handsome, especially if he was in the process of saving her life. Why lie? "Fine. He was the sort you'd think was gorgeous. Broad shoulders and all." Jessica shoved off the counter and headed for her room, where the joy of sweatpants awaited and this conversation ended. "And to make your dreams even better, I'm pretty sure he wasn't a regular Joe from down on the line, not the way he handled himself. But just remember, for all we know, that exterior hid a whole tangle of crazy." Somehow, she doubted that. The way he took authority and dove at her attacker said there was more to him than a man who was simply in the right place at the right time.

"All I heard in that jumble of words was you noticed the color of his eyes." Angie's laugh followed Jessica up the hall to the stairwell. "Maybe you'll see him again."

"Doubtful." At least she hoped not. Any man who stepped on her authority the way he had didn't sit right with her, even if he had saved her life.

Jessica climbed the stairs and shut the door on Angie's amusement, then leaned back against it, letting her body relax for the first time in hours. If she didn't have work to do, she'd crawl into bed right now and will the world away for the rest of the night.

Even though she'd hedged with Angie, it wouldn't be a bad thing to see her anonymous defender again, at least so she could thank him for putting himself in danger on her behalf. If he hadn't been there…

Shuddering, Jessica forced herself to move. Going there

now would just solidify the image and unfurl it in her nightmares later. Not that she needed much help. Even if she didn't have recurring dreams about her last deployment, the decor in her bedroom would agitate her. Why Angie had seen fit to go Gothic in here with deep red walls and heavy dark wood furniture was a mystery Jessica had never felt like solving. She was just happy to live off post.

Changing into track pants and a sweatshirt, Jessica gathered her uniform to toss it into the laundry. Every time she bent to pick up clothes from the hardwood floor, her shoulder pounded a reminder it had only been a few hours since she'd done battle with one of her soldiers, who'd now gone missing.

She snatched up her uniform bottoms, unwilling to think about this day anymore.

Something hard clattered to the floor and slid beneath the dark gray bed skirt. Kneeling to reach with her un-injured arm, Jessica retrieved the object and held it up.

Private Channing's cell phone, the one that had fallen from her backpack when she swung it at Jessica's head. Sinking all the way to the floor, Jessica powered up the device, praying it held enough charge to give her a clue as to what was happening with her disappearing soldier and the attempted theft of yet another laptop.

The phone chimed to life with just under a quarter of its battery showing. Almost immediately, texts popped onto the screen, vibrating the phone and chirping to the point Jessica nearly shoved the thing under a pillow. When the noise finally stopped, over a dozen texts waited.

It was probably an invasion of privacy to read them, but since the girl had lost the phone while swinging a backpack at Jessica's head, privacy really ranked low at this point.

Jessica clicked on the first message. It was nothing but letters and numbers strewn together in a random pattern. Each and every message read the same way, though they came from two different telephone numbers.

Sitting back against the bed, Jessica let the device hang from limp fingers between her knees. It was almost like a child had typed text after text right under their parents' noses. Private Channing didn't have any children and no family that Jessica could remember seeing in her records when she'd arrived last week to prepare for rotation overseas. The woman was a foster child, her next of kin listed as a friend she'd met in basic training.

Lifting the phone again, Jessica clicked out of the messages and hesitated only a moment before going to email. The slight pain in her shoulder urged her past any sense of contrition for snooping.

No new emails, but dozens of already-opened ones sat in the queue, each with an attachment.

Why stop now? Jessica clicked on the first one. No message, but the attachment opened to reveal an official Department of Defense photo of a young male soldier. The next three emails were the same, with dozens more behind them, all sent within the past six weeks. Face after face flicked by, none of them bringing a name to mind, one or two of them vaguely familiar, though it could have been they bore resemblance to a famous person…or her exhaustion was kicking into overdrive.

Jessica turned the phone off and pulled herself up. Likely, Channing had found some weird dating site that catered exclusively to the military. There were worse things young soldiers had done with the Internet, that was for sure.

She slipped the phone into her backpack and pulled out her personal laptop, wanting to sleep but knowing her keyed-up mind wouldn't let her. Lately, her father had started pushing the Green to Gold option on her, hinting he'd like her to take advantage of the Army's program that allowed her to go to college on their dime and become a commissioned officer.

It was tempting, earning her father's respect, but she'd have to temporarily leave behind her status as a medic. The thought burned in her chest. She was already sidelined for a year, watching the home front, helping soldiers transition into and out of the Army, working with the families… Would it be worth it, walking away from her dream career for an even longer stretch of time, simply for the possibility of making her father proud?

She shoved the laptop aside. Researching colleges and ROTC programs would only frustrate her more. She'd be better off staring at the dark ceiling and praying to fall asleep.

Tomorrow, she'd turn the phone over to the military police and let them deal with it and the blue-eyed mystery man who'd saved her life.

The food court of the small shopping center at the Fort Campbell Post Exchange buzzed with hundreds of soldiers and their families, all trying to grab lunch and go. With a lot of the units rotated back home from deployment, the lines were long, and the noise was loud.

Jessica eyed the crowd, watching people mill about as she waited to fill her drink. Too many people in one place. She suppressed a shudder and watched a teenage boy wearing a backpack stride across the room, head down. Her muscles tensed, shoulders aching, as he wove his way through the crowd. It wasn't until he walked out that she relaxed. In combat, backpacks, unattended bags, huge crowds—they all spelled trouble.

She'd been back stateside for five months, but the wariness hadn't left yet. Likely, it never would. She still dodged potholes in the road, still scanned thick groves of trees for evidence of a sniper... Yesterday's events hadn't helped, to be sure.

As the man in front of her stepped away, she pressed her cup to the lever for ice, and then filled it to the brim with sweet tea.

Sipping her drink and hoping in vain the caffeine would waylay the effects of her sleepless night, Jessica turned from the drink machine and surveyed the room, trying to find an empty table with a view of one of the TVs. There. By the front window. If she could just beat the nineteen other people who'd probably spotted it, also. She took two steps from the fountain, and a body collided with hers, knocking her drink from her tray. It splattered to the floor, dousing her lower legs and covering her boots with sweet stickiness.

Cold tea ran inside her boots, soaking the tops of her socks. With a gasp, she stepped back, the cup squishing beneath her heel.

A young soldier stared at her, eyes wide as he took a step back. "Oh man." He shoved a wad of napkins into her hand and retrieved her cup from the floor. "I'm sorry."

Jessica didn't even have to see his rank to know he was a very green private. The dark Army-issued glasses and gangly newborn colt stance told her without needing to see the rank on his chest. "Don't worry about it, Private." It wasn't what she wanted to say, but taking her frustrations out on this poor kid wouldn't help. She knelt and blotted at the drink on her boots, biting back words she'd have to repent for later, she was sure. "I can get another drink. And I have a spare pair of boots in my office." Thankfully.

The kid still looked mortified. Fresh out of basic, he was definitely used to getting yelled out for every minor infraction, and was likely waiting for the tongue-lashing he thought he deserved.

Jessica pulled in a deep breath and straightened. "Really, it's all good."

The private looked down at the cup in his hand. "I'll get you another drink."

He was gone before she could protest that he really didn't have to do that and was somehow back within minutes, even though the lines were still crazy long. Jessica didn't question as he fed ice into her cup. "Um, Staff Sergeant? You missed a spot on your toe." He started to reach down, then nervously pulled his hand back, aiming a finger at her left boot. "You were drinking tea?"

Focused on her shoes, Jessica nodded, and then took the cup he offered before he scampered off with another apology.

With her coveted table by the window now occupied by three soldiers, she picked up her tray and spotted another in the far corner of the room, the angle too sharp to see the TV. Oh well. She didn't need to see the news anyway. She already knew all she needed to know. Her new brigade had shipped out without her, the chain of command claiming she should get more time stateside since she'd only been home a few months before her transfer to Fort Campbell. Her father was disappointed she'd been put in Rear Detachment, refusing to believe it was all about timing and not something she'd done wrong. To him, there was no value in her position. He'd never grasp the need for someone to be on the home front to act as liaison to the families, to support the soldiers who had deployed and to aid the transition for those coming and going overseas.

It was quieter in the corner anyway, away from the crowd. Sliding into the seat, she shoved a straw into her drink and unwrapped her hamburger, glancing at her watch. Half an hour to shove in hot chow and get back to the office before the next briefing.

She reached for her tea as a man slipped into the seat across from hers and laid his hand across the top of the cup. "Don't drink that."

Jessica sat back in her seat, trying to keep her jaw from going slack. The blond, blue-eyed soldier was the same man who'd come to her rescue yesterday—and he had to be out of his mind. "Do I know you, Staff Sergeant?"

"No, but trust me."

Grabbing his wrist, the material of his uniform rough beneath her fingers, she lifted his hand from her drink. After staring down a gun and a knife yesterday, there was no room for fear in the middle of the crowded food court. She didn't have time for this guy, even if he had saved her life, and even if he possessed the bluest eyes she'd ever seen. This current behavior was out-of-bounds. All she wanted was lunch in peace before an afternoon of listening to a commander who liked to hear his own voice. "Worst pickup line ever. You going to tell me next that I'd be better off going with you for drinks somewhere? That you—"

"Your drink's spiked."

"Right." As a female in a predominantly male world, she'd heard every line in the book. This one not only took the cake, it sliced it and shoved it down her throat. "And you're James Bond." She reached defiantly for her sweet tea, but his hand was quicker, drawing the cup to his side of the table.

He couldn't be serious. "What is your problem?"

But there was no amusement on the man's face. His mouth pressed into a straight line, and a fairly recent scar ran from his hairline at his temple back toward his ear. It made him menacing. And deadly serious.

He was either telling the truth, or he was crazy and she should wave over one of the military policemen who tended to be around the Post Exchange for a lunch break.

Leaning forward, he slid her drink to the side. "When you're a female, what's the first rule you follow? Never let your drink out of your sight."

"I didn't." Who was this guy to lecture her?

"You did. Just long enough for your clumsy friend to dump something in it. I watched him."

The private at the drink machines? That kid was about as murderous as a toothless toy poodle. "So why didn't you chase him down?"

"I thought it was more important to keep you from drinking it first. We can pull surveillance video later."

Jessica wasn't buying a word of this. Guys like this, fresh back from deployment, feeling lonely… They were trying to find someone to take their minds off things. She glanced down. No ring. At this moment, her blue-eyed "protector" was nothing more than a lonely single soldier looking for a woman any way he could get one. Somehow, he'd been in the right place at the right time yesterday, maybe because he was already watching her. Grasping her tray, she stood, staring him down. "Keep the drink. I don't need it."

"Sit down, Staff Sergeant."

"Goodbye." She stomped two steps away, but stopped at the sound of his voice.

"Your full name is Jessica Maria Dylan. You were born at Fort Benning, Georgia, to Colonel and Mrs. Eric Dylan. You came to Campbell a few months ago from Fort Lewis, Washington. You're a medic assigned to First Brigade who didn't ship out with your unit because you haven't had enough downtime since your last deployment. On that deployment, you came under fire after your convoy hit an improvised explosive device, but rather than take cover, you went out into the mix and saved two soldiers' lives. When your commander tried to put you in for a commendation, you fought him until he backed down…reluctantly. Oh, and two weeks ago, your government laptop was stolen." When she turned, he tilted his head. "Ready to listen?"

No one but her former commander knew she'd turned down that commendation. And no one but her current chain of command knew her laptop had been stolen once already. "How did you know all of that?"

"It's my job to know that…and to protect you."

Jessica gave up her defiance and sank into her seat, finally deciding to give Staff Sergeant Sean Turner the satisfaction of investigating her drink. She popped the top and glanced inside.

A fine white powder coated the edges of the tea and floated in a sheen across the surface of the liquid. Her hands grew cold, and she shoved the cup away. Her head pounded, threatening nausea. "What's going on?"

Staff Sergeant Turner scanned the immediate area around them, then pulled a folded paper from his pocket. "These are my orders."

Jessica scanned the paper, not recognizing his unit name, but picking up that he was pulling temporary duty for an investigation. She folded the paper and stared at the tight creases. "You're investigating me?"

There was something about his bearing, his attitude. He was Special Forces or deeper. She kept silent, knowing he'd eventually be forced to fill the space with words.

Staff Sergeant Turner pocketed his orders as he lowered his voice. "My unit works to combat groups that hack computers to funnel money and information but who are operating in the physical, as well. Essentially, it's cybercriminals buried in sleeper cells. We're deep because there are times the ones we're investigating are soldiers. We've been looking into a series of laptop heists. The theft of your laptop two weeks ago is the first time we've seen the first theft and been able to anticipate the second. The interesting thing is, there have been chatter spikes each time. I've been watching your machines, and it just so happens our thief came out hot right under my nose yesterday."

As much as she didn't want to believe any of this, his knowledge of her past and his orders spoke to the truth. "So what do you need from me?" Jessica laid a hand on the cell phone in her leg pocket. She hadn't had a chance to turn it over to the MPs yet, and now she wondered if she should.

"Nothing except your trust, and maybe for you to be a second set of eyes." He sat back and laid his hands splayed on the table. Several small scars creased the knuckles. "Staff Sergeant Dylan, this theft is different. You saw both of their faces, and the evidence says they're willing to kill you for it."

"You saw both of their faces, too."

He waved a hand in front of his face. "I'll give you that, but with them making a second attempt on you just now, I'm inclined to believe they think you know something else, too."

"That's why you're operating under the assumption

the kid tried to poison my drink, because they think I know more than I do." Jessica's fingers tightened around the cell phone. She ought to be afraid, but her mind was too busy trying to function under the surreal information Sean Turner was feeding her. "If you can prove that's actually something dangerous in my drink."

"If you'll let me, I can have it analyzed and know within a few days." He leaned closer. "There's more. They were watching your house last night."

She didn't even want to know how he knew that. "I still say you ought to be worried about your own well-being."

"I'm not worried about me."

The words sent a jolt through her that she didn't want to acknowledge. She could take care of herself, but knowing someone else had her back untwisted something in her heart, something she'd rather leave alone. She would do well to remember this man only wanted her trust so he could get to the bottom of his investigation. She swallowed the emotion and made her decision. "You're right. They're not after me because I saw them. Too many other people did, too."

Sean arched an eyebrow but didn't say anything.

"It's probably because I have Channing's cell phone." She started to pull it from her pocket.

"You have it now?" At her nod, Sean reached across the table and grabbed her free hand. "Not here." He stood and scanned the room. "I have to get you back to your battalion. Now."

THREE

Sean ran his hands around the edge of the nondescript brown door, slowing along the top of the frame just in case anyone was stupid enough to leave something incriminating up there.

Nope. Leaning against the beige cinder block wall beside the door, he scanned the tile floor with a curled lip. Barracks sure were better today than when he'd signed up, but nothing beat an apartment of his own. An apartment he'd barely had time to unpack after moving from Maryland to be closer to his new home base in northern Virginia. They'd shipped him out on this assignment in record time, forcing him to leave his new place in a wreck of boxes and half-empty closets.

Thankfully, after Jessica shared Specialist Channing's cell phone with him, she'd trusted him enough to let him accompany her to the battalion. Well, she partially trusted him. She might believe he was who he said he was, but she still wasn't 100 percent convinced her life was in danger.

He'd followed her back to her unit, filling in her commander with the least amount of information he could. Jessica Dylan had already been vetted by his superiors, and they knew she could be trusted. The rest of her unit was still being investigated and had to know as little as possible. There was no way to tell who was involved.

Once he'd obtained permission to be in the building, he'd uploaded the contents of the phone to his laptop while Jessica got clearance from the military police to search Specialist Channing's room. The phone hadn't yielded much on the surface, but he had a lot of decoding ahead of him. While Jessica thought the texts were nothing more than child's play, they nagged at Sean. They seemed more like encryption. The numbers and digits weren't random. In fact, they were the same pattern in many of the messages. As for the emails? Something wasn't right there, either. No one had any reason to carry around that many head shots of soldiers.

That cell phone was the key to proving these laptop thefts were related, that the thieves weren't petty criminals. They'd been mentioned in terrorist chatter, but his unit still felt this was a low-level priority. That's why they'd sent Sean.

He tapped the phone through his pocket. His last mission had brought him into the unit as a consultant, an operative when a desperate situation called for one. As the man who'd uncovered terrorist activity among their contractors, he'd already been in the know about classified intel. He'd just uncovered everything they needed and shipped it back to his best friend, Ashley, in the States when the terror cell blew his cover and took him. Took him and tortured him, trying to discern what he knew.

When the bad guys went after Ashley, his lifelong best friend… That was almost more than he could handle, though it had helped knowing his buddy Ethan Kincaid was protecting her.

His actions overseas had brought him into the unit full-time. But after what he'd been through, sending him out to investigate this mission was proof his superiors thought he wasn't back up to speed, not operating at full capacity. If he were in their boots, he'd probably want him to prove himself, as well. He'd been tortured but not broken, though that last part was debatable. His sleep was still sporadic and restless, peppered with nightmares when it came.

He had to be successful here if they were ever going to trust him with his own team, ever stop thinking of him as the poor sap who'd made a key mistake and found himself taken hostage. He had to prove to them and to himself he was fit for this assignment.

Footsteps pounded on the stairs, and Sean straightened and prepared to fight, but it was Jessica who appeared around the corner. She held out the key to Specialist Channing's room as she got closer. "Captain Alexander said the military police and Criminal Investigations spent a large chunk of yesterday in there, but we're clear to go in now. We probably won't find anything. I'm guessing they took every piece of evidence that even looked like it had any bearing on her thievery."

"Yeah, but they're not looking for the same things I am." He held out his palm for her to lay the key in it, her warm fingers brushing his skin.

The touch telegraphed straight up his arm. There was no doubt Jessica Dylan was a beautiful woman. Her brown eyes were as warm as hot chocolate, and the way that one stubborn length of dark hair kept escaping the bun she'd tried to tame it in made him itch to tuck it back.

Sean shook his head and tightened his fingers around the key, running his thumb down the jagged edge... All things he shouldn't be noticing about her or any other female. She was a witness in need of his protection, his only ally on this investigation. Nothing more. Getting involved with her was against his personal protocol, and he had more than enough to worry about without dragging another woman into his life. He'd almost killed the last one.

Slipping the key into the lock, Sean eased the door open, muscles tensed for action in case someone had beaten them into the room.

There was no intruder, but the room was a disaster. Clothes strewed the floor. Several pizza boxes balanced precariously on the small desk and soda cans overflowed the trash.

Jessica followed, grimacing at the chaos. "Did our guys make this mess, or was Channing this disorganized all along? I've been around a long time, and I've never seen a room in as sad a shape as this one." She fingered a pizza box and watched it slide to the floor. "I mean, I've seen messy soldiers before, but this? There are too many inspections for a soldier to leave a room as trashed as this one. And I'm not sure she was here long enough to merit this kind of disaster."

"You can fault the investigators for part of it." Sean pulled open a duffel bag and dragged a hand through wads of drab olive T-shirts. "But not all of it."

"Maybe because this was her temporary housing, she didn't bother to worry about inspections. She was supposed to ship out in a few days. She just in-processed from Fort Carson a week ago."

"Still, something's not right in here." Sean stopped in the middle of the room and swept the small space. It was a good thing it took more than overflowing garbage to turn his stomach. "What was her rank again?"

"Channing's a Specialist." She'd been in a couple of years and was just above a Private in rank.

Sean pulled the duffel open again, sifting through it

and a smaller bag on the floor beside it, giving in to a growing suspicion as he did. Shoving a heap of detritus from the twin bed, he dropped the clothes onto it, then went to the closet and pulled out all the uniforms there, adding them to the pile.

Jessica stepped back and watched. "What exactly are you doing?"

"Thinking." He pulled random articles of clothing from the bottom of the closet. "At any point in your career, especially when you were a young soldier, did you throw out every single one of your uniforms and start over with used ones?" Sean dumped the clothes onto the bed, then pulled a pair of jump boots from the floor of the closet and tossed them into the mix.

"I'd turn in old uniforms to central issue and get new ones, but usually not all at once. Some of it was used, but not much of it. We got new stuff before deployment, but I kept that back home and wore my old gear overseas. Less I had to buy later. Why?"

Sean swept a hand at the clothes on the bed, waiting to see if he was right or simply thinking sideways. "Tell me what you see."

"A mess." Jessica twisted her lips, but she didn't step back and call him crazy the way she had at the food court. Maybe she was warming up to him.

She'd better. It would make this job a whole lot easier if he didn't have to fight for her trust every step of the way.

After surveying the heap of uniforms for a minute, Jessica lifted an undershirt, then a pair of pants. One by one, she inspected tops and bottoms, setting them to the side and growing more thoughtful with each piece.

She had to see what he saw.

"Sean." She stepped back, stopping spare inches before she backed straight into his chest.

Her warmth eased through his uniform top, forcing him to open up the space between them before he decided he liked the feeling. It hadn't escaped his notice that she'd used his first name. It also hadn't escaped his notice that he liked the sound of it when she did.

Jessica didn't seem aware of his thoughts. "The gear is right, but the clothes… None of them are new. And none of them are Channing's." She turned on her heel, realized how close she stood to him and slid to the side, clearing her throat. "It's all used, even has other people's names on some of them, like she picked up every single bit of it at one of those surplus stores right off post. None of it has been issued to her by the Army." She picked up a patrol cap and ran her index finger along the brim. "This is more than a soldier would need just to travel overseas."

"Exactly." Sean nodded. Her observation skills rivaled some of the best he'd worked with. "Something's going on with your missing soldier, and I'm starting to think we're right that it's a whole lot bigger than the data on your laptop."

Tossing Channing's patrol cap back onto the bed, Jessica walked toward the window that overlooked the parking lot. "I don't know. It seems like a leap to me."

"A leap?" Sean stepped up behind her but kept his distance.

Good for him. She'd gotten a little too close earlier, and while the man might be a conspiracy theorist to the highest degree, he was every good thing Angie had guessed he was and more.

And that made him dangerous.

Jessica didn't turn around. "In reality, I've got a soldier

who has used uniforms and tried to steal my laptop and has now gone missing. I've got a mysterious powder in a cup of sweet tea. And I've got you." Only one of those things was a proven threat.

"You skipped the part where your missing soldier pulled a gun on me while her buddy approached you with a knife." Sean's voice was way too matter-of-fact.

She hadn't forgotten; she just wished she could forget. Refusing to talk about it seemed to be the easiest way to make that happen. "Okay, that, too. But that's all. It seems localized to me." Jessica finally risked turning to face Sean.

He was sitting back against the small desk in the room, arms crossed over his chest. "You forgot the whole reason I'm here."

To be a pain in her neck? "What reason is that, Staff Sergeant?"

His jaw tightened slightly at the use of his rank, but he didn't comment on it. "Chatter. We picked up specific chatter for this unit, for your specific computer. Chatter from known terrorists."

Okay, so there was that. Jessica sank to the edge of the second twin bed. "You really think terrorists were after my laptop? There's nothing on there they can use. No troop movements. No intel. No battle plans. Only thing on there is records and personnel data."

"I think terrorists are after several laptops. Remember, yours isn't the first. It's only the one we were able to get a jump on." He tipped his head to both sides, stretching his neck. "Give me a general idea. If I went on to your laptop today, what would I see?"

"It's in my office, and you can go through it all you want. Channing pitched it when I was chasing her. But

I'll have to sign you in. You'd need my ID card because the laptop has a common access card reader on it."

"You haven't lost your ID have you?"

"Really?" Jessica smirked, then pulled her ID out of her thigh pocket and held it up between two fingers. "I've been around too long for that. And even if they had my ID card, they'd have to get my password to go along with it. I'm sure, if they're the hackers you seem to think they are, they could gain access, but once in there, the most interesting information they'd get for their trouble is my calendar, some general emails, and…" *No. Please not that.*

"What?" Sean straightened, dropping his hands to his sides. "What would they be after on that laptop?"

"With the right information, they could get access to the DD-93s for the unit."

"That's not good."

Jessica dug her fingernails into her palms. No, it wasn't. The form DD-93 was the Record of Emergency Data. It contained contact information for soldiers' next of kin if the worst happened. "There are names and addresses on there. If someone got access to that information, they could locate any soldier's family they wanted." Just the year prior, a local group had terrorized soldiers' families on post in an attempt to bring the men home early. But terrorists? With that information, they could wreak havoc on families and tear down the morale of the entire military.

She consciously relaxed her fingers. "The good news is, they didn't get my laptop."

"But they got your first one…and others from other bases."

"True, but to get access they'd have to know log-in information and passwords for the system and—" she wrinkled her nose "—to be honest, that's risky. It's got to be something else. They could hack that database without calling attention to themselves by stealing laptops. Access can come from any computer, not just a government laptop."

"It's something to think about. Anything else?"

"General information about soldiers. Honestly, whatever you think is on there is what's on there. Your basic information for each of our men and women."

She'd wasted half of her afternoon dealing with Sean Turner and his theories. He kept spouting things she didn't even want to think about and, with her body aching and her mind fogging from lack of sleep, it was better to just be an ostrich, to stick her head in the sand, and pretend everything was normal. "I have to go meet a spouse at the Soldier Center. She lost her ID card and needs someone to hold her hand through the process."

"Isn't that the Family Readiness Group's job?" Sean waved a hand toward the door for Jessica to go ahead of him.

"Normally, but I know the soldier, and his wife felt better calling me than her point of contact. I think there might have been some friction there at one point." She glanced at her watch as she walked out the door, keeping her distance from Sean Turner. This was one favor she was glad to do, especially if it got her out of his presence. "I've got to be over there in half an hour. And then I'm going home to pretend today never happened." She was hosting the college girls from her church for dinner and Bible study tonight. Their chatter and company would be the best thing to happen to her today.

"Let me come with you." Sean pulled the door shut and locked it, then held the key out to Jessica. "I'm not really comfortable with letting you out of my sight after what's happened the past couple of days."

Jessica took the key and pocketed it. "Just when I'm starting to think you might not be so crazy after all, you go and sound like a stalker."

"I'm just saying—"

She held up her hand and headed up the hallway ahead of him. "And I'm just saying. I'm going to the ID card facility and home. Not much can happen between here and there." Well, it could, but she could take care of herself. She'd spent the past ten years proving that, and she'd have to keep proving it if she was going to go Green to Gold, from enlisted to officer.

Sean was going to argue. Jessica just knew it. But before he could, the trill of a cell phone echoed off the cinder block walls.

"Dylan, wait." Sean's voice halted her.

Jessica stopped and turned.

He was holding up Specialist Channing's cell. "It's ringing."

"Answer it." Whoever was calling could know exactly what was going on, could hold the answers that would put Sean Turner on the road and out of her life for good, before she noticed yet again how blue those eyes of his were and how well he wore his uniform.

Sean shook his head. "I'm not taking the chance of tipping somebody off. You recognize the number?"

The phone stopped ringing as Jessica stepped closer. "Bring up the recent calls list."

Sean obliged, but he stopped in midswipe as the phone chimed once. His face tensed and he held out the phone for Jessica to read the screen. "They just wiped the email clean."

"What?" Jessica grabbed the phone and stared at the No Mail message.

"I backed it up, so we haven't lost anything but—"

The phone pinged again, and Jessica flicked the screen to open a new message as Sean eased closer.

Tell Staff Sergeant Turner an old friend says hello.

Sean's mouth pressed into a thin line, the edges whitening. He pulled the phone from her hand to focus on the words.

"What's wrong?" Jessica took a step closer, reaching out to touch his arm, but stood instead with her hand hovering between them. They didn't know each other well enough for her to reach out to him, though every instinct in her urged the contact.

"They know me." His voice scraped over controlled emotions.

"They know your name. It's on your uniform. Anybody who sees you knows it."

He shook his head, finally lifting his gaze to look at her. His eyes were cold, hard. "No. They made a point to mention 'an old friend' in that message…" He stepped back and tensed. "They want me to know they don't only know my name. They know who I am."

FOUR

Somehow they know who I am. It had been two hours, and still Sean's words chased each other in Jessica's head.

As the clock edged closer to five, Jessica settled in her seat, pressing her back hard against the gray plastic. The ID card facility at the Soldier Support Center was hopping with soldiers trying to get minor issues squared away for themselves and their family members.

This was not exactly where she wanted to be right now. As much as she tried to make conversation with the young wife next to her, her mind kept wondering if the analysis on the powder in her drink had come back, if someone was really going to try again to kill her and how the sender of that text message knew Sean Turner.

His composure had cracked at the words, coming back together quickly when he realized she'd noticed. Still, she couldn't forget that look, that quick flash of something she couldn't quite figure out.

Beside her, Ellen Johnson frowned, then smiled slightly. "Thanks for helping me put together all of this paperwork. There are so many hoops to jump through with Garrett deployed. I'm scared to death I'm going to do the wrong thing and someone will yell at me or something."

The young wife was like a dozen others Jessica had met over her time in the Army. Young soldiers, panicking about deployment, would marry their girlfriends, move them on to a new post and leave them for parts around the world almost before the ink was dry on their marriage licenses. Jessica half understood it, that need to have someone waiting at home, that drive to protect the ones they loved by making sure they had the benefit of insurance should anything happen. Still, it always chafed her a bit when the guys did that, because so many wives were still children themselves, barely eighteen and pulled away from their families to live in a strange place while they worried daily about the men they loved. Some of them, like Ellen, might have been better off staying home with their parents during the deployment. The dream of making a home with a young soldier was often a whole lot more romantic than the reality.

Jessica shoved aside her thoughts and prayed they didn't read on her face. She dragged the toe of her boot across the dark flecks in the floor as she sat taller. "You're not the first to lose an ID card while her husband is away." Murphy's Law always seemed to kick in when the soldiers left, with something—or someone—getting lost or broken almost immediately. "I'm just glad I was able to help."

"You didn't have to stay and wait with me. I know this isn't exactly under your job description." The younger woman pushed straight blond hair behind her ear and smiled, her gray eyes not quite receiving the message. "I appreciate it. I'm not quite sure what all of the drama with my point of contact was, but she didn't make me very comfortable asking her questions." Ellen stopped to listen as another number was called, then tightened her hold on the boho purse in her lap. "It's intimidating here, all of these soldiers in one place."

"Friction happens. Where'd you grow up?"

"Michigan. Not exactly a lot of military bases up there." Ellen waved a hand that encompassed the whole room, then dropped it back into her lap. "This is a totally different world, not just the Army and the South, but being married and everything."

"I'll bet."

"I'll be okay if you leave when they call me back."

Jessica fought the urge to check her watch. The girls in her Bible study would get to her house around seven o'clock, and if she had any prayer of having dinner ready, she'd have to get out of here in the next fifteen minutes. Still, the last thing she ever wanted to do was telegraph that impatience to Ellen. "Are you sure?"

"When I'm done, I can walk right out of here that way." She pointed to a door behind them. "I just go through those doors and I'm home free for the lobby and the parking lot, right?"

Jessica nodded. "Right." She surveyed the room, unable to shake the feeling that had plagued her for the past ten minutes, as if eyes she couldn't see were watching her. She was probably just jumpy after the past two days and her time with Sean Turner. The things he was saying were incredible, but the more he talked, the more she found herself believing him.

It didn't help that she was remembering more details about yesterday. Either that or she was dreaming. It had better not be the latter. If she wasn't careful, she'd start having nightmares. She shuddered and caught her lower lip between her teeth, letting go just as quickly. Projecting weakness was one of those things she hated the most, and biting her lip was a tell for sure. Her father had chastised her for it often.

She sat taller, much preferring the vision of Sean Turner's blue eyes to the dark, menacing ones of the man who'd approached her with a knife. She shouldn't think of the Staff Sergeant that way, though. There was a wariness to him, a way that he had of seeming vigilant at all times. Turner had trouble written all over him; she just couldn't pinpoint why.

Best not to think about those eyes or that incredibly cute just-over-regulation-length dirty blond hair of his. It wasn't often, even with the Special Forces unit on Campbell, that she got to see a guy with actual hair on his head.

Tossing her head, Jessica surveyed the few people still waiting in the rows of gray chairs as the clock ticked nearer to close of business. At the reception window, a man turned his head quickly, the motion catching her eye. She stared hard, waiting for him to turn back around. Did she know him? Something about the brief glimpse of his face was vaguely familiar. She ran through a roster of the soldiers in her unit, but none seemed to fit his description, and besides, the majority of them were deployed.

He glanced back at her again, giving her a better view of his face as his dark eyes met hers, glittering in recognition. Rather than hail her, though, he stared hard, seeming to memorize the lines on her face. Even from across the room, he chilled the blood just beneath her skin.

As if confirming something in his mind, he turned from her, then walked away, straight across the room and out the door.

The tension in her muscles relaxed. Her imagination was hyped into overdrive today. Although she couldn't shake the feeling she'd seen that man before, the image was right on the edge of her memory yet refusing to gel.

Ellen stood, breaking Jessica's concentration, and lifted her purse as she tilted her head to the oversize TV screen above the door that led to the main ID facility. "My number just came up. I go through that door, right?"

Jessica stood. "Yep. Are you sure you don't want me to go back with you."

"I'm fine now. It was just kind of nerve-racking at first, afraid I'd do the wrong thing after they turned me away and told me I needed more paperwork last time." She reached to give Jessica a sideways hug, then stopped, opting for a small wave instead. "Thank you, Staff Sergeant Dylan. You're a lifesaver." Ellen was gone before the words were fully out of her mouth.

Not for the first time, a sparse loneliness brushed Jessica's heart. She felt so out of place sometimes as a woman on an Army post. Pulling her beret from her side leg pocket, she ran it through her fingers and headed up the hallway toward the exit. Sure she had friends, but whenever she put on the uniform, something seemed to happen. Other women never seemed to know how to react around her, seemed to forget she was a female who'd appreciate a hug and girl talk just as much as the rest of them. Just because she was a soldier, it didn't make her any less of a woman.

Though the balance was tough. She had to be strong enough to hang with the boys but woman enough to be one of the girls. She pressed her lips together as she pushed out the door into the cold, gray fall afternoon, grinding her black beret tight onto her head. On days like today, when her life was spinning in strange directions and she wanted to do the perceived "girl" thing and break down over all that had happened, the tightrope was even harder to walk.

At the end of the duty day on the Tuesday before

Thanksgiving, the parking lot was virtually empty, only a handful of other cars filling the spaces. It appeared everybody else wanted what she wanted. Home.

She checked her watch again as she headed for the far end of the parking lot. If she could get there in the next half hour, dinner for her Bible study girls would be right on schedule. It would take a run of green lights to get her that far that fast, though. Some days, living closer to post would be a blessing.

Pulling her keys from her pocket, Jessica clicked the door locks on her small gray sedan, her steps slowing as she drew closer. The car click of the locks was muted, the sound it made when it was already unlocked. She vividly remembered locking it because a young private had jumped ten feet in the air when the horn blasted as she did. Normally, she wouldn't think twice but today—something seemed off, that gut feeling she often got when things in her world just weren't right.

Then again, her radar had to be out of whack with Sean Turner feeding her ghost stories. That man was messing with her head in more ways than one. Shaking off the chill that tried to claw up her spine, Jessica pulled open the car door and glanced into the backseat as the lights illuminated the interior.

A man crouched low behind the driver's seat. Dark eyes glittered at her, more chilling than the air, the same eyes that had been locked on her in the waiting room. He lunged over the seat toward her, grasping the edge of her sleeve and pulling her forward.

Jessica's shoulder collided with the side of the car, the jolt to her already-injured muscles arcing through her to steal her breath. Her throat closed, trapping the scream that swelled and fought to escape. Digging in her heels, Jessica used her height advantage and threw her body backward, momentum causing her to stagger to the ground as the rough fabric of her uniform slipped through the man's fingers. She hit hard, jarring her teeth together, scrambling to get up before the man could exit her vehicle and keep her down for good.

The car door pushed open as Jessica rose to her knees, but another body charged in from her left, foot clipping her knee and buckling her helpless to the ground.

Sean dove at the door, catching it with his hands and landing on his side as it slammed shut on Jessica's attacker. He rolled to his feet as the man in the vehicle scrambled out the passenger door and got a running start, Sean's boots skidding on loose gravel as he scrambled up to pursue.

The man leaped into a small SUV that sat waiting, door open and engine running, and skidded out of the parking lot as Sean pitched sideways to keep from being hit, sliding along the ground on his still-healing shoulder. He fought the intense desire to curl up against the pain, struggling to read the license plate of the fleeing vehicle. He was on his knees when Jessica thudded up beside him.

Sean reached for his phone to call the military police, and then abandoned the idea within the next second. The gate to get off post was too close to their position. Before he got through to anyone, that vehicle would be long gone, and all he'd have was more attention turned on Jessica when this investigation still needed to be under wraps. Without knowing who was involved, he couldn't call in help unless he needed backup or had a suspect in custody. He abandoned the idea and turned his attention to Jessica.

She was pale, the hand she held out to him shaking.

He wanted to ignore the help, to prove that he could

do this all by himself, but he knew it would insult her if he didn't accept it. The thread that held them together was tenuous enough already, and protecting it was worth the perceived bruise to his ego.

She helped haul him to his feet as he winced against the pressure on his shoulder. Her gaze went there immediately, her hand following to rest on his upper arm. "Are you hurt?"

"Old injury." He shook off the warmth of her fingers before he could decide he liked it and turned the focus back where it belonged—on her. "Are you okay? What just happened?"

"I opened my car door, and he was in there." The statement might have been matter-of-fact, but the tension around her mouth telegraphed that this had upset her more than she was letting on. "I had the situation under control. Where did you come from?"

From his car five spaces away from hers, but that probably wasn't the right thing to say at the moment, not with Jessica bound and determined to take care of herself.

He didn't have to say a thing anyway. Her expression hardened. "You're following me?"

"And aren't you glad?" Seriously. She could at least be a little bit appreciative that he'd saved her life. Again.

"I'd be happier if you hadn't let the guy get away."

The words were born more out of adrenaline than malice and Sean knew it, but they still cut. Had he been more vigilant, he'd have seen the warning signs. Had he been quicker, he'd have arrived in time to see the guy crawl into her car, not three minutes before she left the building.

Then again, had he been three minutes later...

He shook off the thought of Jessica dead in the parking lot with a broken neck, a stab wound or worse. He'd made it in time. She just needed to understand how vital it was for someone to have her back. If this didn't convince her the danger was real, protecting her and getting to the bottom of this mess was only going to get harder.

Reaching out to lay a hand on her arm, he turned her toward his car. "Let's get out of the middle of the parking lot. You can wait in my truck while I clear your vehicle."

She stopped, pulling away from his grasp. "Wait?" She threw a hand out toward Clarksville. "No. I have dinner tonight for the college girls in my Bible study. We get together before Thanksgiving and—"

"Whoa." Sean held up a hand to stop the flow of words. She'd lost her mind if she thought she was going to up and leave a crime scene before they'd done all they could do to catch the man who likely would have killed her. "No leaving until the techs get here. And no Bible study at all, not until we know you're safe."

She opened her mouth to protest, but he shook his head. "Cancel it. The last thing you need is to put someone else in danger because they're at your house when the bad guys show up. I can't let you do that."

Her mouth closed, and she at least appeared to be considering his words. Denial could be stronger than common sense sometimes. In Jessica's case, it seemed she carried a pretty hefty dose.

Unfortunately, Sean knew what a superhero complex coupled with denial could get you. A space in the hot seat staring a terrorist square in the eye. He'd rightly earned that seat by ignoring the signs that had led to his own kidnapping. He wasn't going to let Jessica do the same, not if he could save her.

Rather than reach for her arm and get rebuffed, Sean

swept his hand toward his rental car. "I'd feel a whole lot better if you weren't standing in the open right now."

He expected her to argue, but she fell into step beside him and crossed the remaining thirty yards to his vehicle. Just a short distance from the vehicle, she stopped. "I know that guy from somewhere."

Sean looked around but saw no one in the parking lot. "Which guy?"

"The one in my car."

"Wait." Sean stopped, pinning his hands to her shoulders so she'd look at him and not away as she had a habit of doing when she was cornered. "You know him?"

"I don't know his name, but he was in the ID card facility earlier when I was there and I wish…" She shook her head and balled her fists again, which seemed to be her trademark move when she was frustrated.

Or scared.

Sean watched her eyes as she talked. This had her spooked more than she would ever let on. Jessica Dylan did not have everything as held together as she tried to make it appear, but with her driven need to prove herself, she'd never give him the satisfaction of seeing her crumble.

Fighting the totally inexplicable urge to draw her close, an urge brought on by her unexpected vulnerability, Sean dropped his hands and took a step back. "You wish what?"

"Nothing. Just that I could figure out where I've seen him before today."

"So this isn't the first time you've encountered this guy?" If the man had been following her before the incident yesterday, it was for certain this operation was much bigger and Jessica wasn't a random target. "Think. Where?"

"I don't know. That's what's bugging me. I've seen him, but my mind won't place him. I've run through everywhere I've been for the past week and can't picture him in any of those places."

"Describe him. Tell me everything about when you spotted him inside, anything you remember about him, no matter how insignificant. His appearance, what he was doing, everything." Before Sean took one more step, he needed to know what he was up against. Even though he'd had a brief glimpse of the suspect, he wanted to hear her details, see if having her talk would trigger another memory.

"Not very tall. My height maybe. Light brown hair. Tanned skin. He looked like…" She pulled in a gasp, reaching for Sean, eyes widening with something close to excitement. "He's on the cell phone."

"What?"

"His photo was in Channing's email. That's why he seemed familiar. I'm sure of it. It's one of the first emails, one of the oldest." She grabbed his wrist, animated once again. "If you can let me see the backup you made of that phone before they deleted the emails, I'll recognize him."

She'd recognize the man, but would it do them any good? Each attack came closer to stealing Jessica and, if the pattern continued, when it happened again, he might not be able to reach her in time.

FIVE

"Something else is going on here." Sean dragged a hand down his face and glanced at the clock in his rental car as he sat in Jessica's driveway talking to his team leader. It was just past six in the evening, and he was already flagging. If he didn't get sleep soon, there was no telling how much longer he'd be able to run on fumes. It hadn't been that long ago when he could make it through a forty-eight-hour stretch without batting an eye, but those days were gone after the events of last spring made him feel a whole lot older than his thirty years and made sleep harder to come by.

He grimaced. Stupid nightmares were not going to keep him from what he wanted out of life. He'd beat them the same way he'd beaten every other challenge. With stubborn willpower.

Willpower that wasn't keeping his emotions out of this thing with Jessica Dylan. She was getting into his head already, and that was definitely not something he was used to. Needing some time to adjust to her presence, he'd cleared the house and let her go in for some time to herself while he made the call to headquarters.

"Tell me what you've got." A clatter punctuated Captain Ethan Kincaid's words. He was either on speaker or headphones. Likely headphones. The man never stopped moving even to have a conversation.

"The guy who came after her yesterday… He was more intent on silencing her than saving his hide."

"You're sure?"

"I know the look." A loud bang cracked on the line, and Sean grimaced, pulling the phone away from his ear. "What are you doing?"

The silence grew long and loud before Ethan finally cleared his throat. "Dishes."

Sean coughed to cover a laugh, then gave up and let the grin sound in his voice. "The one-man destroyer of terror cells is doing dishes?"

"Knock it off, Turner." Even Ethan sounded amused. "That terror cell wouldn't have come down without you and Ashley. And you deserve more of the credit than the rest of us."

Sean frowned. Last year at this time, he'd been in Afghanistan, gathering intelligence on a terror cell led by an American contractor, Sam Mina. Things had gone south quickly in the spring, and Sean's best friend, Ashley Colson, ended up in the crosshairs because of his decision to pull her into the mission. It was a choice that nearly got them both killed.

"I know what you're thinking. Stop beating yourself up." All amusement vanished from Ethan's voice. "Mina's in jail. The cell he led has fallen apart. You're safe. And believe me, Ashley is more than fine." Ethan should know. He'd married her two months ago.

Sean cleared his throat, shoving the conversation aside. He didn't want to talk about the past. All he had was the future, and even it was on a shaky foundation. "Ashley's more than fine because she talked you into doing housework. Tell me again why you're doing the dishes, Kincaid?"

For a minute, it seemed Ethan wasn't going to take the bait, but he finally spoke. "She's all spun up because my parents will be here for Thanksgiving, and she spent the entire day making pies. Oh, and that was after she ferreted out a hacker in Turkey. You know. Typical Ashley day."

There was nothing typical about Ethan's wife. Sean could testify to that. He had known her his whole life. Sean might count himself a master at data encryption, but when it came to everything else about computers, Ashley Colson Kincaid beat him without even having to fight.

"Speaking of her hacker tracking ability, I need her to remote in to Staff Sergeant Dylan's desktop computer. If she saw Channing downloading data, I want to know what it was. If Ashley and I sift through it together, we have a better chance of finding something."

"Done. Just be careful not to tip your hand to the mission. If we're right and this is a terror cell, we don't know who's involved. Get with Ashley and set up a time. Think you need me to put a team together for you and send them out there?"

For a half second, Sean considered the offer, but he rejected it. Having only recently been cleared for full duty after his injuries, he hadn't had a chance to vet and put together his own team. "After what your partner did, I'm not sure I trust anyone I haven't personally selected, and you're wrapped up in your own mission."

"Mitch was one guy."

"One guy who nearly managed to tear down the entire unit." Their Special Missions Unit was working at skeleton status, rerunning background checks on each member after Craig Mitchum sold out to be Sam Mina's inside man. Trusted team leaders like Ethan and Sean were spread thin as the unit regrouped, each doing the work of three men.

"Do me a favor, Sean. Remember you're down there to see if this thing has legs, not to show you can handle an entire mission all by yourself. Don't get in too deep trying to prove something."

Sean clamped his back teeth together. Ethan Kincaid might be one of the people closest to him, but the man had no idea what it felt like to be helpless, unable to save yourself or the person you loved most in the world. If this mission blew up and Sean succeeded in bringing down another cell, it would prove he could do this job, would finally confirm to himself that he was truly past all that had happened in Afghanistan, that he wasn't a failure and a danger to the people he cared about.

"I know you heard me say that." Ethan was more stubborn than Sean gave him credit for.

"I heard you. Have any suggestions?"

Ethan's exhale was loud in the microphone. "Tate's out there in the wind, itching for something to do. Do you trust him?"

Though officially retired from the Army, Tate Walker acted as their jack-of-all-trades, their go-to guy when things went sideways. He'd lost his home and his identity while working to save Ethan and Ashley and now spent his time tucked away, building a new facade of a life. Aside from Ethan himself, Tate was the one guy Sean knew wouldn't turn on him. "Call him in." He'd breathe easier knowing someone had his back.

"Done. Based on his last location, he should be there in a few hours, but keep him close. He's too valuable to us undercover to let anybody see him out there too much."

Sean rolled his shoulder, trying to stretch the knot that

persisted there. "I've let Specialist Dylan know what's going on, so she's clued in to the investigation. She's shaken up a little, but she refuses to admit it."

"You're certain they were going to kill her?"

"Positive. They've made two overt attempts, and I had a buddy at a local lab test her drink." Dropping off the sample was why he'd nearly been too late to save her at the Soldier Center. "It was tetramine."

Ethan whistled low. "Rat poison out of China? That stuff's a hundred times worse than cyanide. What made your buddy test for that?"

"Apparently, it's making a comeback." Sean held tight to the bottom of the steering wheel. "These guys aren't playing. They'll come after her again. We've got to be vigilant."

"You're in front of her house, aren't you?" Ethan's voice rang with conviction.

"Why would you say—"

"Knowing you, I'd expect no less. Just don't let the neighbors catch you haunting the driveway."

The light turned on in one of the upstairs rooms. Ethan hinted Sean was acting like a stalker, but knowing Jessica was in danger drove him to watch out for her as best as he could. If she died because he let his guard down... Well, that wasn't an option.

He let his fingers knead the muscles in his neck as he surveyed the front of her house again. The two-story just a few blocks from the Cumberland River boasted a turret and a wide covered wraparound porch with enough rockers to seat an entire team of soldiers, but what Sean really needed was a clear view of the privacy-fenced backyard. "I'll keep an eye on Staff Sergeant Dylan while you guys see if you can find anything about our attackers. One is in those emails I forwarded to Ashley. I'll tag which one."

"Sounds like a plan." Ethan was back to his all-business self. "Keep me posted."

"Make sure you don't get dishpan hands." Sean killed the call without waiting for Ethan to respond.

He tossed the phone onto the passenger seat and frowned at the silence, staring at the radio. He'd promised Jessica half an hour before he invaded the privacy of her home, and he had fifteen minutes of that time left. It would be nice if he could turn on music and fill the cavernous silence of the small vehicle with noise. Then he could keep back the memories that liked to creep up in the silence, but the radio would only mask any outside sounds he needed to hear.

No. He'd have to sit here in the quiet and try not to think.

Headlights turned from one of the side streets and headed slowly toward him. Sean slid lower, trying to make himself as small as possible, though, from his angle in the driveway and with the darkness settled in, it would be hard for anyone to see him. No need to get excited yet. This time of day it was likely a soldier coming home from duty or a nine-to-fiver headed home from work.

As the car came closer, it slowed in front of Jessica's house as though the driver was searching for something. The vehicle crept past the house, then hung a U-turn, passing the house slowly again before it sped off down the street.

Sean sat taller and tapped his thumb against his thigh. It could be nothing, but he couldn't shake the feeling he wasn't the only one keeping an eye on Jessica Dylan.

Jessica shut her bedroom door slowly to keep from slamming it hard enough to crack the frame. The day had been too much like a bad action movie. She was hungry, tired…

And scared. Her fingertips pressed into the wood of the door. Everything had been just fine until she'd climbed into her car and Sean had shut the door for her, then turned and walked to his own car to follow her home. No matter how hard she'd tried, she couldn't stop staring into the rearview, waiting for a head to pop up.

And she was furious. At some point on the drive home, the shock of the day's events had worn off and the anger had kicked in. Who was this Sean Turner to think she was a damsel in distress in need of his protection anyway? The fear might be real, but in every single situation she'd been in, no matter how frightening, she could have saved herself. She owned a gun. She'd been taught to defend herself the same as he had. She'd been in combat. The last thing she needed was a knight in shining armor to come to her rescue. She might be a female, but she was also a soldier, and she was going to go downstairs and tell him exactly that. He couldn't control her life, and she didn't need one more male judging her every action. Changing into jeans and her University of Tennessee sweatshirt, Jessica pulled herself together to go into battle.

She focused on the fact he'd called her pastor behind her back and canceled her Bible study dinner. This arrogance of his was going to be the end of him. Or of her.

Aside from needing the company of her friends, she needed the outlet that preparing dinner would give her. The precise measurement of ingredients, an end result she could control. It was the only order to be found in this new chaos.

And Sean Turner had taken it away from her.

She stalked down the stairs and found him coming in

the side door. "It's one thing to interfere with my job. It's a whole other thing to stick your jump-booted toe into my personal life." The man had done nothing but turn her life six degrees from sideways. There was no telling why she bothered to let him into her house other than her Southern grandmother's teaching.

He choked, probably swallowing a laugh at her ire. Whatever. He could think what he wanted. Unless he thought she somehow needed him. In spite of his superhero tactics, she didn't need his help. "No jump boots tonight, but they're in my car if that makes it easier for you to view me as the Grinch who stole your social life."

No, he wasn't wearing jump boots tonight. The jeans and lightweight black sweater he wore did a whole lot more for his looks than the drab Army combat uniform had.

Had her mind really gone there? She'd groan out loud if the man wasn't standing in her entryway waiting for her to indicate where he should step next. So much for her grandmother's hospitality. "Tell me again why you feel the need to be here?" Yep. Granny Josephine was rolling in her grave.

"After all that's happened today, my chain of command thought it was best if you weren't alone."

Jessica refused to let him see her shudder, to let him see how much that man in her vehicle had affected her. In spite of her ire, she had to admit if Sean wasn't here, she'd curl into a ball and have a good hysterical cry. If Sean hadn't been stalk-protecting her, she'd likely be on a slab with her throat slashed. Her fingers went to her neck instinctively, feeling for blood.

Sean stepped closer and wrapped his thumb and index finger lightly around her wrist, pulling her hand from her neck. His voice lowered to a depth she'd not heard in the time she'd been forced into his presence. "You're safe, and I'm going to make sure you stay that way if you'll let me."

For the slightest second, Jessica wanted to lean forward and lay her head on that strong shoulder, let somebody else bear the load. She took a step closer, shrinking the space between them until she could feel the warmth he radiated.

For a moment, he hesitated, then slipped his arm around her and pulled her closer, the embrace comforting.

She sank into it, feeling a comfort she couldn't describe, a small thrill running through her.

But then she stiffened and pulled away, straightening her shoulders. She was a soldier same as he was, and there was no way she was going to let him think he was stronger, not even for one millisecond. It would only give him a reason to rain condescension on her.

Still, as much as she hated to acknowledge it, having him around took the edge off her fear. It was good to know there was someone else around, someone who could see what she couldn't. He was growing on her.

And that irked her more than anything else.

She stalked across the hardwood entry toward the kitchen at the back of the house, shaking and refusing to admit why. "So I guess that means I'm stuck with you until my roommate gets home?"

His footsteps echoed close behind. "You've got a nice place here. As for your Bible study, I didn't think it would be wise to have half a dozen young women here as sitting ducks. You want to take the risk of one of them being taken hostage while they walk to their car?"

His words trailed off so slowly, Jessica turned to see if he was still behind her. He was, though the look in his eye said he'd left the room for somewhere else altogether.

Figured. He'd charged into her life, ripped it apart and now probably couldn't stop thinking about last night's football scores.

Still, what he said made sense. Sadly, there was a lot she could say right now, but unfortunately it all started with *You're right*.

She snatched three of the packages of chicken breasts from the refrigerator and tossed them into the freezer before retrieving the smallest package and throwing it onto the counter with a sickening thud. She pulled out a tomato to dice. Sooner or later, she'd have to admit her ire was more at the situation than at Sean Turner.

For now, it felt too good to have a punching bag.

She ran her knife through the tomato, trying to put mismatched pieces of events together. They had no idea why that soldier's picture had been on Channing's phone. No idea how he'd recognized her. And no idea why he thought her presence was worthy of a violent, lonely death in the parking lot of the Soldier Center.

Jessica swallowed hard, needing to know her throat was still in one piece. Sean was right, even if she'd never stoop so low as to tell him so. She cleared her throat. "So, you're going to invite yourself to my house for how long?"

He didn't answer, just relaxed against the counter on the other side of the sink and planted his hands on the granite. "You know you're basically cooking dinner for one tonight, unless your roommate's going to be here. Why are you still hacking at those tomatoes like I'm going to change my mind and issue everybody in your Bible study engraved invitations to come anyway?"

"You're here. You're planning on staying for some undetermined amount of time. You might as well eat." Not to mention cooking was her safe place. The actions of slicing and sautéing took her back to long evenings in the kitchen, girl talking with her mother as they made prime rib or homemade lasagna. In the kitchen, Jessica was in control. If a dish fell to pieces, it was her fault, the result of something she alone had done. The outcome lay firmly in her hands.

Jessica laid the knife beside the cutting board and turned to face the man who'd invaded her workplace and now her home. "You do eat, don't you? Or are you some kind of robot who runs on solar power and sass?"

One perfect eyebrow arched. "Even superheroes have to eat sometime."

Oh man, he was cocky. But she'd fed him the line so it shouldn't surprise her he'd run with the metaphor. If he was anyone else, she'd have laughed. But Sean Turner? No way she'd give him the satisfaction. Earlier today, she'd thought it would be possible for them to work together. But now, after his command and conquer tactics with her personal life, he should consider himself blessed she was cooking his dinner and not throwing it at him. He should have involved her, not gone behind her back in a way that hinted she was too stupid to make phone calls herself.

Sean tipped a chin toward her work. "What is all of that anyway? It doesn't seem one bit like real food."

It was Jessica's turn to lift an eyebrow. She held up the package of meat. "You can't tell me you've never eaten chicken before."

"Breaded and deep-fried."

"You're kidding." She tossed the package back to the counter, opting for a clinical recitation of the dinner menu over considering the spark in his eye as he teased her. "We're having bruschetta chicken breasts, an Italian salad and buttered fresh noodles from one of the Italian restaurants in town." Only because she hadn't had time to make her own. Boy, Turner would really dive off the deep end when he found out noodles came from something other than a box at the grocery store.

"It's so obvious you were about to feed a bunch of women."

Jessica didn't have to see him to know he'd rolled his eyes. She scooped the tomatoes into a bowl, rinsed her hands and stacked the basil leaves. Rolling them into a tight spiral, she ran the knife through the herbs. "Didn't your mom feed you? Or did she leave you to your own devices to hit the drive-through every night?"

There was a long period of silence—so long Jessica wondered how deeply she'd shoved her foot into her mouth. Finally, he spoke. "I grew up outdoors with my dad. Spent winter mornings in a tree stand hunting deer and summers knee-deep in a river fishing for trout. My mom could throw together a venison stew like you can't even imagine. She believed in good food with thick gravy and cream of mushroom soup. There was no girlie *broo*-whatever that is you're making. She'd feed you breakfast so packed with waffles and eggs and bacon at four in the morning that you wouldn't even think about food again until you came out of the woods at four in the afternoon." He cleared his throat, as if some emotion hung up the next words. "There's not near enough protein in those vegetables you're tossing together."

Jessica dumped the basil into the bowl with the tomatoes and pulled the balsamic from the cabinet above her head, careful not to look sideways at the enigma in her kitchen. He'd shifted from all-business soldier to all-loving family man.

Something about the way he said those words revealed he loved his mother more than he would ever tell her, but there was a heaviness that hinted at loss, too. It tugged at her heart in a way that shouldn't happen when it came to a man like Sean Turner. She angled the subject away from that emotion. "And what do you eat now? Besides breaded and fried chicken flesh of indeterminate origin?"

"Indeterminate origin? I know where my food comes from. The drive-through. You should drag that chicken through some flour and fry it. You do that and move out of my way and I'll show you how to make a mean sawmill gravy. Then we'll talk about some real eating."

"Absolutely not." No way was she risking her daily physical training calories on a heart attack like the one he'd described. "Have your mom make you some next time you're home. I'm sure she'd be happy to contribute to your elevated cholesterol numbers."

Sean didn't answer. There was a shuffle and a soft sound. When Jessica turned, he was gone.

SIX

Sean stood at the small front window, hands braced high on the sides of the frame, fingers digging into the wood so hard his forearms strained. He stared out at the darkness that swallowed the front yard, hardly seeing anything for the red of his anger.

Not at Jessica. She'd been doing her level best to bond with him or something, trying to draw him out, he guessed, and make him talk like a normal person. And it had all been okay. She was actually kind of cute and sarcastic in a way he really shouldn't notice, not if he was going to do his job.

No. The anger he felt had nothing to do with her and everything to do with himself. He was weak. Ever since Ethan Kincaid and an FBI hostage rescue team had freed him from terrorists who'd snatched him right out of his own office in Afghanistan, emotions about his parents' deaths had ridden way too close to the surface. He'd always been able to tamp them down and beat them back with more work, more training, more focus. But now, at night, his dreams alternated between vivid memories of his captivity and horrifying images of what his parents' last moments must have been like.

Times like this reinforced why he never talked about

them. In those rare moments in the past when he'd let himself be vulnerable, it had always been with Ashley. With her, he'd felt like the strong one, even though he was hurting, too. Her parents had died in that fiery crash right along with his, and it was usually together that they grieved. They'd been best friends their whole lives, had even survived a short engagement born out of his brotherly need to protect her. Thankfully, they'd realized quickly that the kind of love they shared was deep, but it wasn't the marrying kind. While Sean fully celebrated the joy Ashley had found with Ethan, it left him with nowhere to turn.

So when Jessica had stepped closer, needing him, pulling her near had seemed too natural. She'd fit against his chest so perfectly, and he'd almost sunk into that moment.

Stupid. She'd been right to pull away, and he should have been the one to do it. Should have never closed that gap in the first place. He had to be stronger than this.

Sooner or later, he'd defeat this weakness and remember the man he was supposed to be, the soldier who had everything together, who won battles and exposed terrorists instead of being sidelined by weak emotion and silly nightmares.

"Turner?" Jessica's voice was more tentative than he'd heard it before, even when she'd faced her attackers.

There was definitely no way he was going to let her be the stronger of the two of them, and no way he was letting any more personal information invade the space he needed to do his job. Pushing off the window frame, Sean slid the curtains closed. He turned and crossed his arms, determined to project the strength of the man he should be.

Jessica stood at the entrance to the kitchen, wiping her hands on a white dish towel, watching him with furrowed brows. He'd worried her, and the fact nearly pushed him over the edge. Why should she care about him? And why did he want her to?

Sean sniffed, the decade-old hurt suddenly too fresh. "My parents were killed by a drunk driver not long after I joined the Army." He dug his fingers harder into his biceps. Hadn't he just decided not to confide in her anymore? The last thing he wanted was her sympathy, or to open up to her in any kind of personal way. It was out of the bounds of this mission and definitely out of the bounds of his life. He'd already lost one woman he thought he'd loved. He sure didn't need another one stepping in to try to take her place.

To her credit, Jessica didn't react. Instead, she stood in place and drew the towel between her fingers. "That stinks. It really does."

The bold plainness of that statement spoke more sincerity than if she'd offered sympathy or condolences. It was real, more real than anything anyone had ever said to him, and it clutched him around the heart in a way he both longed for and hated. "Yeah, well." He shrugged and tried not to watch what she did next.

She lifted a mischievous smile. "You know, if it would make you feel better, I could always slap a whole stick of butter in the frying pan and dredge that chicken through some flour and some heavy-duty seasonings. You know, give it a real Southern country kitchen kind of vibe. Or I could swim it in some good ole melted shortening and make your heart scream for mercy. How does that sound?"

Sean choked on a laugh that felt better than anything else he'd done in the past seven months. It made him appreciate the woman in front of him more than he should.

With that smirk on her face and her hair down out

of its usual low twist, man, Jessica Dylan was cute. She caught something in his gut that swirled as hunger never had, twisting him up in a way that was totally uncomfortable and more exhilarating than jumping out of an airplane with an oxygen mask at thirty thousand feet.

Ashley had never made him feel this way. The thing that had existed between them had been a steady rock under his feet, built on a shared upbringing and shared grief. Ashley had been a safe place to land. This? This was dangerous. A landing zone in the middle of an enemy-controlled airfield.

Either that or the idea of breaded and pan-fried chicken was making his palms sweat. Yeah. He was a man. Food had that effect on him, right?

"Well?" Jessica was waiting for an answer, threading the dish towel between her fingers as she eyed him, as if she was trying to read his mind but wasn't really sure she wanted to know what lurked in there.

"Tell you what." The frame of the window pressed into his spine as he leaned back, trying to appear nonchalant while his muscles fought to remain clenched. "You make me this froufrou tomato whatever chicken of yours tonight, since you already got it started. Next time, I'll slap a big ole steak in some flour and fix you a country-fried, gravy-soaked slab of meat that will make you decide cholesterol and fat are absolutely worth the years they'll shave off of your life."

Her eyes slid to the side, and she held the towel tighter between her fingers, something in his words throwing off her confidence.

Next time. He'd all but invited her out on a date with the word picture he'd just painted. Man, he needed to check himself before he wound up in the ditch. An organization with all the markings of a rogue terror cell was on the loose and they were trying to kill the woman in front of him. He'd do better to remember that than to think of how he could wrangle another meal with her.

"Know what?" He straightened and dropped his hands to his sides. "You go make the rest of your dinner. I'm going to walk around your house inside and out and make sure there's nothing to be worried about. It's better if I know the lay of the land anyway in case something happens." He took a step toward the door, the twinge in his shoulder reminding him he wasn't all of the man he was pretending to be, that little bit of pain reigniting the passion in him to take down any bad guy who stood in his way.

Without looking back at Jessica or waiting for an answer, he crossed the room for the door and stepped out, pulling the door shut behind him, reveling in the autumn chill that frosted his emotions and reminded him that all he needed was his mind. His heart could stay cold.

The warm scent of browned butter drifted over Jessica, cut by the pure acid of the tomatoes and basil in the bowl beside the stove. She pulled the last of the lightly fried chicken from the cast-iron skillet and set a thick, perfectly browned piece on each plate, sliding the third one into a plastic container for Angie to eat later. She always stayed out late on Bible study nights, but Jessica never gave up hope that one day, the younger woman would decide to sit in.

Sean had been prowling around for half an hour, but she hadn't missed the expression on his face before he left. Something was bothering him, and it was more than his parents' deaths.

She scooped buttered noodles from the strainer at the sink. Sean Turner wasn't being 100 percent honest with her, and it rankled, even though she had no right to know details about his private life. He owed her nothing other than to complete the mission he'd been assigned. Still, standing there watching him hold on to the window frame as though he could pull it from the wall, something in her had wanted to go to him, to give him comfort for whatever had him so angry it reddened the back of his neck and whitened his knuckles. He was hurting, and everything in her wanted to fix it.

It was good he'd walked out, even though it sliced a little at her spirit. He was on a mission for a unit she didn't completely understand. He was not her friend and he was definitely not date material. If she was ever going to prove to her father she was a good soldier, no man could be date material. She had to stay focused.

Carrying the food to the small kitchen table, she analyzed the green cloth and white plates. Maybe she should have ordered pizza instead. Cooking for him was too intimate, and the implication that he'd return the favor one day? Well, that never should have set her heart racing.

Sean Turner was in dangerous water.

She was filling two glasses with ice when the front door opened and his heavy footfalls sounded on the hardwood. He didn't come immediately into the kitchen, but she found him standing at the entrance, waiting for permission.

Carrying two glasses to the table, she waited for him to speak, then took matters into her own hands. "Find anything?"

He stepped closer to the table, pulling his hands from his pockets and rubbing them together against what was bound to be a fairly chilly, damp Tennessee fall evening. "I'm not sure I like how the covered porch wraps all the way around to the back. Too much cover. You've got a sturdy privacy fence, but there's a weak spot at the back corner. If you've got a hammer and a few nails, I'll tighten it up after we eat, make it harder for anyone to slip through."

The glass clattered against the table harder than Jessica intended. The idea of someone sneaking into her backyard grated on nerves still raw from her encounter that afternoon. It was terrible for someone to lie in wait in the back of her vehicle. It was a whole other horrifying thing for them to gain entrance to her house while she slept. "You think that will be enough?" She caught the tip of her tongue between her teeth as she set the other glass down. The question made her sound like a weak female. She was a soldier. A soldier with a concealed carry permit, a revolver and combatives training. There was nothing to be afraid of.

Except there was. For the first time, the idea of Sean Turner bunking on her couch outweighed the goal of getting him out of her life as fast as possible. She'd never wanted a man to protect her before, but tonight it sounded like the only way she was going to get any rest was if someone helped pull guard duty.

Sean stepped to her side. The warmth of him filtered through her sweatshirt. It was best not to turn and face him.

"I shouldn't have muscled in on your private life like I did earlier today. You're a strong woman. So strong you scare me." He fiddled with a napkin on the table as if he wasn't used to making apologies and wasn't exactly sure which way to turn next. "I'm sorry."

The way he stood so close and the unexpected humility in his words tore apart the last of her anger. She relaxed. "Thank you."

"Still, you can't do this on your own. I've got my stuff

in the car, and all I have to go back to is a hotel room where I'll sit up all night anyway. Keeping watch here is better than trying to explain to my chain of command why I didn't stand guard. Rather than face that music, I'll sit out in my car until the neighbors call the cops and label me a stalker. I doubt either one of us wants that one on our record."

Jessica flashed a quick smile in spite of herself. She straightened a plate on the table, some stubborn part of her still not able to surrender. "True. But I don't want the girls in my Bible study getting wind that a man spent the night at my house." There was too much she couldn't explain to impressionable women younger than her, some of whom held her up as an example, although they definitely shouldn't.

"Your roommate will be here. Everything's on the up-and-up."

"My roommate's only here until Wednesday. She's going to Knoxville to visit her parents for Thanksgiving."

"Well, hopefully this won't take that long." He pointed to the front room. "It's the couch or your driveway, but I'm not walking away when some guy was hanging out in your backseat this afternoon. I can promise you he wasn't there to tell you you're due for an oil change."

That was a low blow, reminding her of that. But it also kept her from arguing any further. "I wouldn't make a dog sleep in the car. I certainly won't make you."

Sean actually laughed. "Well, at least I rank one higher than the dog."

"We can hash this out later." Jessica stepped away and pointed to the table. "We should eat before the food gets cold."

Without arguing anymore, Sean stepped to the small

table and waited for her to choose a seat before he sat in the one across from her.

She winced as her foot brushed his. Probably would have been better to sit at the dining room table. Then she could have put him at one end and herself at the other. At least there wouldn't be the constant danger of accidental footsies. She tilted her knees to the side and drew her feet under her chair, bowing her head to pray silently. She didn't know where Sean's attitude toward God lay, but she wasn't going to change her routine for him.

When she lifted her head, he was watching her. "You pray."

"You're surprised? You're the one who canceled my Bible study, remember? How about you?" Why the answer to that question interested her so much, she had no idea.

"I'm sure you'll never let me forget." He slipped his napkin into his lap, noticing his plate for the first time. He poked the chicken with his fork. "You fried this?" Without lifting his head, he raised his gaze to meet hers. "For me?"

It was Jessica's turn to shrug. He hadn't answered her question, but with the way he was watching her now, it seemed too personal anyway. "It's a panfry, not anything deep and greasy like your local fast-food joint. You seemed like you could use a pick-me-up." Great. Now she'd acknowledged she recognized his emotions and cared he had them. If he kept hanging around, she was going to get deeper until the surface vanished.

His chin lifted. "Thank you." Before she could respond, he dug his fork in and started eating.

The words were simple, but they tugged at Jessica's heart with an intimacy she hadn't felt in a long time. Well, ever, if she wanted to be honest. But not toward

Sean Turner. He was here to keep tabs on her and whatever was going on at her unit, nothing more. He'd be gone soon, away from any perceived emotions. She just had to keep herself in check.

Still, dinner would be awkward if nobody spoke at all. She pushed a tomato across her plate. "From your accent, I'm guessing you're not from around here."

"I'm a Yankee through and through." He forked a bite of chicken into his mouth and nodded with an arched eyebrow as he chewed before swallowing. "Good chicken, Dylan. I'm from upstate New York, not far from Fort Drum."

"And you ran around outdoors like a wild child?" It wasn't hard to imagine him as a boy, covered from head to toe in dirt, or as a young man, all dressed in hunting camo, waiting patiently in a tree stand. The picture was knee weakening, almost as much as the image he cut in a uniform today.

Man, she needed help. Jessica shoved a forkful of pasta into her mouth to keep her thoughts from leaking out uncontrollably. She probably wasn't the first girl to develop a crush on the guy who'd saved her life—or on Sean Turner. That was all it was, even though she wasn't usually given to that particular ailment.

Sean slid his plate closer. "Wild child? Not so much. My mom would have none of that. But I did spend a lot of time in the woods with my dad and Ashley's dad. If we ever go back to the Dark Ages, I can hunt and field dress pretty much all of the meat you'll ever need."

There was that name again. *Ashley.* She must be important as much as he talked about her. It shouldn't surprise her to know a guy who looked like Sean Turner already had a woman waiting for him. And it shouldn't make her heart sink, either. "You aced that part of training, then."

"Survival? Without a hitch. I was the most well-fed soldier in my class. My platoon practically wrote poetry to me."

"Yeah. Okay." There it was again, that cocky sense of humor that was starting to grow on her. *God, help me. I don't need to fall for this guy.*

"How about you?" Sean turned the tables in her direction. "What are your parents like?"

Reaching for her water, Jessica schooled her reaction. As an Army brat with a high-brass father, she'd learned long ago to be diplomatic. "My dad is a retired colonel. My mom is the consummate officer's wife. She taught me how to cook."

"She did a good job."

Jessica would not blush at his praise. "Thanks."

"Beats pizza, which is what I'd have ordered tonight."

Well, then. Even if it meant she had to keep her feet under her chair to keep from making contact with him, she was glad she'd nixed the pizza idea. Cooking had made her feel better, and it had unlocked something in Sean that she was grateful to see. A humanity that softened him. It made her want to know more about the man across from her. "This your first mission with your unit?"

Sean opened his mouth, then closed it again. "You know, I'd prefer if we—"

A crash from the side yard dragged Sean to his feet as he threw his fork onto his plate with a clatter.

Jessica rose with him, but he'd stepped around the table, shielding her from some invisible adversary. How he'd produced the pistol in his hand so fast was beyond her. "Kill the lights and get under the table."

Was he serious? Hide in her own house like a refugee from a bad spy movie? "You've got to be—"

He shoved her toward the table, away from the sound.

"Don't argue with me. Do it." He reached for the light switch, plunging the room into darkness. "The last thing I need to do is shoot you in the dark or hesitate when the bad guy steps up." Without waiting to see if she obeyed, probably assuming that she would, he stalked for the den where that light shortly went out, too.

SEVEN

Sean crept up the hallway toward the end of the house where the crash had originated, hoping against hope that Jessica had done as he'd told her to do. If she was half as stubborn as he thought she was, the chances weren't good. He'd have to be double sure of his aim if he needed to pull the trigger.

With his back against the wall, he held his gun at the ready and crept toward the bathroom at the end of the short hallway, grateful he could carry his weapon off post without having to reveal his mission. On post, the hoops he'd have to jump through would compromise the unit's need for anonymity at any cost.

If he and God were on speaking terms, Sean would thank Him for Jessica's comments about his parents that had driven him to explore the house earlier. To his left lay a small office with a desk and a sofa, and to his right, a laundry room with a door that led to the back porch. Stairs leading up to three bedrooms were just past that. At the end of the hall, there was a full bath with a bathtub surrounded by a shower curtain. That was where the sound had come from.

He searched his mind for the contents of the room. An older house, this one featured a small window over the tub and facing the side yard, likely built to allow light into the small space. Tucked on the side of the house, that had to be the point of entry. Slight scrapes echoed on the tile as Sean crept closer, vision adjusting to the dark.

The shower curtain moved, and a figure stepped out, a dark silhouette against the dim light from the window. Sean didn't wait but holstered his gun and drove into the figure with his good shoulder, knocking the person backward against the counter, catching the unsuspecting intruder in the lower back on the edge of the granite. The figure cried out, going limp for a moment before he fought back with a vengeance, a strong punch catching Sean in the temple.

It took all Sean had not to loosen his hold and back away, which was surely what the man wanted. Instead, he held tighter, leaned back slightly, and rushed the intruder into the cabinet again, driving one hand up to smash the man's upper body sideways against the medicine cabinet that jutted out from the wall beside the sink.

The figure crumpled, dead weight in Sean's arms, but Sean didn't let go. For all he knew, the guy was playing possum, waiting for Sean to let down his guard so he could unleash a surprise attack.

When the man didn't move for a solid minute, Sean released him to slump to the floor. Flooding the room with light from the switch, he pulled his pistol from his hip and aimed it squarely at the attacker. "Call the police," he yelled back to Jessica. "Tell them we have an intruder in your home and you need law enforcement and an ambulance."

To her credit and Sean's surprise, Jessica didn't question, and it was only seconds before he heard her relaying information to the operator.

Keeping his gun level on the intruder, Sean toed him over in the small space to get a good look at his face.

A bruise was already forming on the side of the man's face and blood trickled out of a cut beside his eye, but it was the same man who'd hidden in Jessica's vehicle at the ID card facility. He was younger than Sean had first thought.

Whoever these people were, they weren't giving up easily. It had been a bold move to wait in Jessica's car, bolder still to break into the house with Sean's vehicle sitting in the driveway.

Sean's breaths quickened as the adrenaline ebbed. What was the scheme that made them so desperate to silence Jessica? Too many people knew Channing's identity already, and they had to know she'd already handed over the cell phone. They'd taunted him specifically in the text message. His grip on the pistol tightened as footsteps came up the hall behind him.

"The police are on the way." Jessica stepped up behind him, staying a few feet back up the hallway, an act of serious self-restraint if he'd ever seen one.

Finally convinced the man was down for the count, Sean holstered his weapon and rolled him onto his stomach to zip-tie his hands and then his feet.

"Are you always this prepared?" Jessica's voice sounded laced with skepticism and not a trace of fear. She tended to stay calm in the moment, he'd already seen, but he also knew she'd been close to tears at some point. The red of her eyes when she'd let him in the house spoke more than words could.

"Only when I've already had to save an asset's life three times."

Jessica shook her head, then peeked around him at the man lying trussed on her bathroom floor. Her head tilted, expression darkening. "That's the man who was hiding in my car."

Sean gave a slight nod, watching her face. She was afraid, he could see it on her face, but she wasn't about to give in and weaken in front of him.

She walked up the hallway, stopping at the closed door that led to the laundry room, careful to keep her back to him. Her shoulders were a straight line, a wall that kept him from stepping closer. Most likely, she didn't want him to see she was terrified. That was nothing to be ashamed of. Three attempts on her life in two days would rattle even the most battle-worn vet, especially on home soil where it was supposed to be safe.

For the first time in a very long time, Sean felt the urge to pull a woman close and comfort her, but Jessica Dylan had made clear she wanted to keep him at a distance, and no matter what he felt, distance was necessary if he was going to put his life and his career back together.

Jessica's shoulders rose and fell. "We've caught him. It's over. You can go to your hotel now and get some sleep in a real bed and not on my couch."

"Are you forgetting you were attacked at your company and someone tried to poison you?"

Her spine stiffened. "You don't know that it was poison yet."

Sean winced. He'd wanted to hold that information from her until things slowed down and the shock from everything else wore off.

She turned. "I said, you don't know that it was poison yet." The repeated words sounded iced with an emotion Sean couldn't identify.

"It was. I got a verbal confirmation." He kept his voice even and his focus on the suspect lying on the floor. He hadn't wanted to add to the pressure by telling her, but he wasn't going to lie. "If you need the full lab report, I can have it for you tomorrow."

Something like fear crossed her face, chased by an impassive mask she carefully settled into place. Her chin lifted. "I still say you have your man and we can get back to our lives."

Was she in denial? "You know better. You're a smarter soldier than that. Specialist Channing is still out there. So is her buddy. This guy here is probably one of many on their payroll or, more likely, all three of them are on someone else's payroll. And as soon as whoever they're all working for finds out we have one of their men in custody, they'll send more. This isn't over." He stared down at the man on the floor and pressed two fingers to his aching temple. "It's only just begun."

Poison.

Jessica stood at the end of the bed and held tight to the dark wood of the antique post, the grooves in the woodwork pressing the soft flesh on her palm. Downstairs, EMTs had removed her unwanted guest, and a handful of police processed the crime scene that used to be her guest bathroom. Somewhere in the house, Sean stood in the middle of everything, likely trying to direct the authorities as only he could.

Upstairs, Jessica leaned against the bedpost as if it was the last solid thing in her world. For all she knew, it was.

Poison. It wasn't surprising. In light of a man in her car and in her house, it wasn't even the most frightening thing that had happened in the past forty-eight hours, but it was enough to wake her up from denial.

Someone wanted her dead.

She pressed her forehead against her knuckles and

stared at the polished hardwood floor. How was she ever going to get out of this one?

"Care to tell me what's going on here?" Angie stepped through the door into the bedroom.

Jessica stepped away from the railing and shoved her hands into her sweatshirt pockets, unable to tell if her roommate was amused or angry. "Wish I could."

"I had to show my driver's license to get into my own house. I haven't seen that many police since... Well, ever." Angie sat down on the edge of the bed and looked up at Jessica, a rare seriousness settling around her. "What happened?"

Jessica had no idea how much she was allowed to say, but she owed her roommate something. "Someone broke into the house tonight and, long story short, the staff sergeant who jumped in yesterday at the company caught him."

Angie tugged at her earring and seemed to try to read Jessica's mind. Finally, she sighed. "It's a good thing you have my trust, because I know that's not the whole story."

"It's the whole story I can tell you right now."

"Well, then, it's also a good thing I'm leaving in the morning to go spend Thanksgiving with my parents, or I'd move us both into a hotel." She smoothed her skirt and stood, giving Jessica a sympathetic hug. "You're sure you're going to be okay?"

Before Jessica could answer, the rapid-fire trumpets of reveille blasted through the room. Jessica jumped, adrenaline surging into her fingertips. Why now? Did God really think she could handle all of this at one time, because she had news for Him... She couldn't. Of all the things that had happened today, somehow hearing her father's ringtone felt like the final straw.

Even Angie knew what was coming. She tossed a

wave and backed out of the room. "I'm going to go hide out in my room and pretend none of this is going on."

Jessica wished she could leave right along with her roommate. Pulling herself taller, she pressed the screen to answer and pulled the phone to her ear, waiting for the volcano to erupt. "Hello."

"Jessica Maria. You tell me right now why I just got pulled away from the dinner your mother cooked for General Alan Marks. You had better have a very good reason for the police officers currently swarming your house." Her father, Colonel Eric Dylan, never disappointed. She should have known he'd be on the line as soon as the first sirens wailed.

Jessica sank to the edge of the bed and flipped on the light that perched on the nightstand, desperate for some cheer to push back the darkness. *It's been an unbelievable two days, but I'm fine, Dad. Thanks for asking about my welfare first.* "How did you find out?"

"Does it matter?"

Not really. There was only one person who could have played tattletale. Her neighbor down the street, Retired Major Dan White. Her father had grown up with Dan, had served with him in Iraq in the early nineties. For some reason, the major felt the need to keep her father apprised of Jessica's every move, likely to prevent her from soiling the precious Dylan military legacy. Emergency personnel at the house would definitely merit a code red call since lights and sirens were a concrete indicator Jessica had made a mess of something.

Jessica pinched the bridge of her nose and sighed. It was probably better to give her father as little of the story as possible. If she told him everything, they'd be here all night while he picked apart each incident and let her know how much she'd failed him and her entire country. "Just a break-in. Everything's okay now."

"A break-in." The colonel's voice fell flat, heavy with disappointment. Jessica could see him pacing the back patio of their massive house in upstate Virginia, fist clenched, veins bulging in his forehead. "Someone broke into your house."

"Yes, but I'm fine, and they didn't—"

"Jessica. You can't even protect your own property. How do you ever expect to lead even the smallest team of soldiers? You have to be vigilant at all times, ready for anything. Security is a top priority. If this had been on a forward operating base and that burglar had been a terrorist, you'd have dead soldiers right now. Pay attention to your surroundings."

"I was. We stopped him just after he made it through the window. He didn't even make it out of the bathroom. And the police have him in custody now."

"Who is *we*? Certainly not you and that flighty roommate of yours. The two of you couldn't stop a spider from spinning a web in the corner of your kitchen."

Jessica winced. The disgust was expected, but the word *we* was a pronoun she never should have used. Her father would jump on Sean's presence like a rabid dog. "I had a friend over."

"Well, I hope your friend is a more competent soldier than you are. Sounds like it, if the burglar's been subdued." The phone muffled for a moment, then her father was back. "I have to go. The general thinks he can put in a good word for your brother and get him a position at the Pentagon. I don't appreciate this call interrupting that discussion. Try to keep yourself out of trouble. The last thing we need is for you to jeopardize your brother's future with your incompetence." The call ended, just like that, the same way it always did.

Jessica threw the phone at the burgundy pillows on the head of her bed and clenched her fists, shaking them out just as quickly. Her mother always said she looked like her father when she did that. Long ago, Jessica had managed to eradicate his mannerisms from her nervous habits, but whenever she was angry, he somehow seemed to crop up in her stance.

"Bad news?"

The voice from the doorway jerked her head up. Sean stood there, leaning against the frame, arms crossed over his chest in what must be his typical pose.

For the smallest of seconds, she wanted to unload everything on him, to pour out how angry, how hurt, the conversation with her father had left her. But no. Never. Like her father, he probably thought she was weak, too. He'd proven it when he told her to stay back while he took care of the problem.

She shouldn't have. She should have followed him up the hallway and been right there with him to take down the intruder in her house. It was her home, her sanctuary to protect, after all. Not his.

"Dylan, are you okay?" He'd straightened, arms at his sides as if he was ready to take on another attacker for her, as if she needed his protection.

Well, she needed no such thing. "Everything's fine. That was my father. The neighbor down the street called and told him the police were here and he wanted to see why."

"Your neighbor. Major White?"

"You met him?" It figured the man wouldn't be content with simply tattling to her father. He'd have to come down to make sure he had the full story and to see the damage for himself.

"Gave him my number to call in case he sees anything suspicious."

Jessica groaned. *Really?* "Great. The major knows there's a man at my house now. I'll get another phone call from my father any second."

"That's a bad thing?"

"Let's just say one more call from the colonel will make too many for one day."

"He just wanted to make sure you were okay, right?"

Why would Sean ask that question? Maybe he somehow knew what had pounded her ears from the other end of the phone line. Maybe he agreed with her father and thought she needed supervision. Well, she wouldn't dignify that with a response. "Are the police done? Do they need another statement from me?"

"The police just left." Sean eyed her, eyebrows drawn together as though he was trying to read her expression, but then his face relaxed in a way that suggested he was settling in for a friendly chat. "Dads can be funny about their daughters. Believe me. I've seen it. Ashley's dad could be a beast."

Yeah, dads could be funny, but definitely not in the way Sean was thinking. She smoothed an imaginary wrinkle out of the bedspread, suddenly aware that she was standing in her bedroom talking to this virtual stranger. Had she thrown all of her dirty clothes into the hamper? It took all of her willpower not to turn and make sure. "Did you need something?"

"You disappeared. I wanted to make sure you were okay. It's been a rough couple of days, and I just dumped more on you downstairs."

That was an understatement. Jessica traced a scratch

in the bedpost. It was easier to focus on the scar in the wood than the man standing in her doorway. "I'm fine."

"Okay, then. I'm going to go dig through the information I downloaded from Channing's cell phone." He stepped back from the door, then rocked forward again. "And if you see a strange man lurking around tonight, I've got backup coming in. His name's Tate."

Great. All she needed was more strange men for her father to get wind of. "Anyone else I should know about?"

"No, but you might want to warn your roommate that Tate and I will be around."

Jessica sank to the edge of the bed, the weight of everything making the air in the room heavier. She hadn't even thought about filling Angie in on the fact there would be a man sleeping on her couch, hadn't really made the decision to let him stay in the house until two minutes ago. After what just happened, there was no reason to argue. "I'll go tell her. And if your friend needs a place to sleep, put him in the office downstairs. There's a daybed in there."

"Thanks." Sean smiled and tipped his head forward. "I'll see you in the morning. And hopefully I'll have some answers for you from Channing's data by then." He started to walk away again.

But something in Jessica wasn't quite ready for him to leave. She needed one more minute of inane small talk in order to acclimate to whatever this new normal was. "You spend all day following me around and all night working going over evidence? You have to sleep sometime, don't you?"

His features darkened, but he quickly reset his bland expression. "Are you an only child?"

Well, that was abrupt, especially considering her father's behavior two minutes ago. She didn't want to talk about it, but politeness kicked in anyway. She brushed imaginary lint off her sleeve. "I have an older brother. A ranger stationed at Fort Benning. The pride and joy of the family." Now why had she said that? It was sure to throw wide-open the door to more questions.

Sean's demeanor didn't change. "I'm an only child, but I grew up close to another family whose daughter was like my sister." Something flashed in his eyes, but then he looked right back at her with that same benign expression. "I'll be downstairs on the couch if you need me. Better warn your roommate." He started to back away and then stopped as though he had an afterthought. "You're a good soldier, Dylan. Very good. I've seen your file, talked to your previous chains of command. I know the awards you've won. You were born to be a leader. Your record said that over and over. Don't let anyone ever tell you different." Without waiting for a response, he disappeared, his heavy footfalls echoing in the hallway.

She'd only known Sean Turner for two days. If he could see that, why couldn't her father?

EIGHT

The light from his laptop glowed soft in the darkened living room. Sean glanced at the corner of the screen. Straight up two o'clock. Dropping his head onto the back of the couch, he stared up at the ceiling, where shadows danced in the dim light. He'd sorted the data from the cell phone and sent it off to Ashley to analyze. Too brain scrambled to do more than give the photos a cursory check, he'd set the laptop to the side, where it mocked him for being too worn-out to do his job.

Once his mind got used to the creaks and pops of the older house, the place was almost too quiet, off the main drag near the river. On the one hand, he'd be able to hear any little noise out of place. On the other, he couldn't stop straining to hear sounds in the silence.

Tate had arrived around midnight and, after a brief rundown from Sean, had taken up a position outside. The mere fact he was out there keeping watch dropped Sean's blood pressure and eased the tension in his neck muscles. He hadn't even realized how much burden he was hauling around until help showed up.

The creaks from upstairs had stopped about an hour ago, and Sean hoped yet again that Jessica would be able to get some rest, even if he couldn't. Her roommate had come home to the swirl of a police swarm. The woman had said very little, just hustled upstairs with Jessica while casting curious glances at Sean. That was fine. He was out of words for the day. He'd spent all of them on Jessica Dylan.

He'd never opened up about his parents to anyone before, not in the detail he had to Jessica. To be honest, the only person he ever talked to at all was Ashley, and now that she was happily married to Ethan, those conversations had all but halted. His two closest friends had paired off with each other and, while he was happy for them, it left him with nowhere to turn.

That was fine, particularly as Sean tried to regain his center. He kept mostly to himself, all business, especially now with the hot breath of the past singeing his neck. But there was something about Jessica that made her feel familiar and safe, even though they'd only known each other a short time.

And that something meant he'd have to be careful. He had an investigation to conduct, and she was in need of his protection because of that.

Besides, his life was too intense to ask anyone else to join him in it.

Sean fought the drowsiness. He'd passed exhausted hours ago, when the adrenaline crash nearly pulled him to his knees, but every single time his brain let down its guard, the memories leaped up. The scars on the tender flesh inside his arms seared. The skin in his shoulder burned at the entry and the exit wound.

He woke up sweating, shaking off the certainty that when he came to full consciousness he'd still be in the captivity of men with hate in their eyes.

Certain that Ashley would be dead and it would be all his fault.

The same thing happened every time, so his body had started rejecting that moment. His mind was always on guard, unwilling to relax. Always listening. Always cataloging his environment, protecting him from the changes he should have seen that day, from the attack he should have anticipated.

The one he could have stopped if he hadn't let his confidence swell into arrogance.

How long could a man live on power naps before his body gave up on him, too?

He'd just forced himself awake again when two quick, light raps sounded at the door. A pause, then four more.

Sean sat up and stared at the small, arched entryway to the house. Surely he'd heard that wrong, but then it came again, only slightly louder this time. Two. A pause. Four.

Tate.

Grabbing his gun from the coffee table beside his computer, Sean crept toward the door and peeked out the small window at the side.

Tate Walker stood silhouetted in the light from the porch across the street.

Sean pulled the door open, then stood aside to make room for Tate to enter. "What brings you inside? Everything okay?"

"Everything's fine. I've walked the whole yard for the past two hours." Tate smiled the lazy grin he was famous for and slipped in past Sean. "What are you doing awake? I told myself I'd knock twice, then go on my way. You ought to be getting your beauty sleep, Turner. You could use as much as you can get."

Sean fought the urge to slug Tate in the arm, but the good-natured ribbing lightened the load that had been sitting on his chest for most of the night. With another person to talk to, the memories tended to recede, hiding out in the dark until Sean was alone again. "Speak for yourself." He flipped on the small tableside lamp, knowing from the layout of the house that the light would never reach upstairs. Still, he kept his voice low, unwilling to risk frightening either of the women he hoped were getting some much-needed rest.

Tate dropped onto the couch and dragged a hand back through his dark hair, already salted, though he was only a handful of years older than Sean. "I honestly thought you'd be sleeping."

"Had a few things I had to get done." He didn't confess the insomnia to anybody. They'd question his mission readiness, and he wasn't ready to defend himself. He was fine. Most of the time. "Thought you were watching the perimeter."

"It's dead quiet out there." Tate stretched his legs out under the table. "I've been all over the yard, saw that spot where you fixed the fence after the cops left. Nobody's coming through there again." He yawned. "My guess is, with the police swarming the house earlier tonight and both of our cars sitting in the driveway, nobody's going to touch this place for the near future."

That was probably true, but it didn't help Sean relax. Sometimes, it was in the quiet that the worst danger lurked.

Tate tipped his head toward the laptop on the coffee table. "Find anything interesting?"

Sean stopped at the end of the couch and surveyed the room, a small space holding a leather couch and a matching recliner that faced a TV mounted on the wall. He wished he dared turn it on for company but hated to risk waking Jessica. "Trying. Jessica Dylan had a cell phone belonging to one of our suspects. I sent the contents to Ashley, though I'd imagine she's racked out for the night by now. I peeked through it, but so far all I've found on it are Department of Defense photos of a few dozen soldiers and some encrypted texts. They make no sense. Either that or I'm too tired to function."

Tate pulled the laptop closer and flicked the touch pad to wake the screen, making a search of the files himself. "So you're still not sleeping?"

The question iced Sean's veins. How did he know? "What's that supposed to mean?"

Tate slid the computer onto the table and sat back again, stretching his feet out and settling in.

He kept his mouth shut until Sean stepped around and looked him square in the eye. "What exactly does that mean, Walker?"

"Snippy much?" The levity of Tate's tone didn't match the question. He tapped a palm against his chest. "Remember who you're talking to, buddy. I didn't sleep the first six months either, and my ordeal was over a whole lot faster than yours."

"Depends on how you define *over*." Sean sank to the edge of the recliner at an angle to Tate. He couldn't lie to the man who'd suffered as much as he had. It would be the height of disrespect. Sean's captivity was longer than Tate's attack, but the repercussions for Tate had been much worse. Sean hadn't lost his entire career. Yet. "Every time I close my eyes, man…"

"You see it all again."

"And feel it." Even saying the words made the scars burn.

"No shame there." Tate stretched and settled deeper into the chair. "I was just getting my head on straight when Stephanie took off and decided she wanted a divorce. Something about that empty bed made everything a thousand times worse. I could actually feel the hollow space in my chest."

Sean winced. During a takedown of a drug smuggling operation at the New Cumberland Army Depot, Tate's cover had been compromised. A suspect with a knife had nearly ended Tate's life, and the ensuing recovery robbed him of his career and his marriage.

Sean had endured a lot, but his struggle was nothing compared to Tate's. He fought the urge to bury his head in his hands and hide from his friend's words. He ought to be over this by now, plain and simple, yet it was seven months later and the night still found him fighting for equilibrium, feeling as if his sanity was a thinly stretched wire.

I'm so weak. Tate managed to get over it. Even Ashley's doing better. Am I going to live through this only to lose everything in the aftermath?

Jessica pushed open the door to her office and refused to admit to herself she let out a sigh of relief when everything seemed to be where she'd left it yesterday. The neat stacks of files still sat at right angles on her desk. Her black fleece jacket still hung on the back of her chair. Her computer still sat in its spot. Tension flowed out of her too-tight muscles as she acknowledged the small part of her that was terrified her office had been violated along with her home.

Or that someone would pop out of a hiding place to grab her. She resisted the urge to look around the door when she opened it, not wanting to give Sean the satisfaction of knowing she was even the least bit afraid. She'd already had to physically stand between him and the door to keep him from entering before her. Jessica wasn't in the market for a bodyguard. She could take care of herself, but she was rapidly running out of safe havens.

Sean, however, had no problem peeking at the space behind the door as he stepped into the room. "I still don't like this." Making his opinion known wasn't something he had a problem with, either. He'd told her multiple times over breakfast how much he didn't like the fact she was putting herself out in the world for everyone to see.

While the two of them bickered, Angie had finally left the table with her bowl of cereal and disappeared upstairs to her room, griping about "mom and dad" fighting.

Even that hadn't stopped Sean. He had only dialed it back when Jessica agreed to let him do the driving.

"I'm just as safe here as I am in my house. I think we proved that last night." Jessica slung her backpack to the floor beside her desk chair and braced her hands on the back of the chair, unwilling to admit the idea left her a little bit rattled. If she wasn't safe at home, she really wasn't safe anywhere. "Staff duty is right next door in the headquarters building. The commander is in his office over there, too. If you have better things to do, I'll be fine by myself here. Doing my job. You know, that thing the Army pays me to do."

"Yeah. The guys on staff duty did a fine job of keeping Specialist Channing in line on Monday." Sean wasn't even fazed by her heavy dose of sarcasm, returning it bite for bite. Instead of dignifying her nasty attitude with any further response, he gestured toward the wall-to-wall windows to his left. "You're a sitting duck in here."

"So close the blinds." She bit the words off. "Whoever these people are, they haven't shown any proclivity for using snipers. Seems their weapon of choice is an eight-inch blade." Jessica dug her fingernails into the black cloth of her chair, willing a shudder away. Somehow, a bullet she never heard coming seemed preferable to a knife to the neck.

Maybe having Sean follow her everywhere wasn't such a bad idea after all. "When will you get to question the man from my house?"

"As soon as the police are done with him and I get clearance. You can't just waltz in and talk to a suspect without authorization, especially in my line of work. There's only so much I can say without tipping my hand. If we don't know how deep this goes, we don't know who to trust. Even your chain of command only knows the bare bones."

Made sense, but it sure did slow down the answers they needed, answers that could put her life back to rights and send Sean Turner off on his next mission before he scrambled her brain any more than he already had.

Jessica dropped into her chair and shuffled a few papers on the scratched wooden desktop, picking up a note that the commander must have dropped off after Jessica left for the ID card facility yesterday. "Specialist Murphy's memorial service is going to be in Iowa. The casualty assistance officer is already on point for his great-aunt. She's the only family he had."

"You had a casualty?"

"Found out about it Monday morning. I was coming back from the notification brief when I walked in on Channing. Monday wasn't the greatest day in the world."

Sean winced. "Sorry."

"You didn't do anything other than show up at the right time. Did I thank you for that yet?" If she hadn't, she'd sure thought it. Or dreamed it. She'd surprisingly been able to sleep last night, largely because she knew Sean was downstairs keeping an eye on the place. Contrary to what she'd expected, she'd slept like a private after twenty-four-hour duty.

"You fried your fancy chicken last night for my dinner. That's thanks enough," Sean said. "It wasn't half-bad, even if you didn't dump any gravy on it."

"I'll take that as a compliment." Jessica grinned and turned on her desktop computer, slipping her ID card into the reader and typing in her password. "I guess we need to change seats if you're going to get over here and do whatever it is you need to do."

As Sean picked up his backpack, she gathered up a handful of items she'd need to work. They rounded the desk at the same time, meeting on the narrow end. Both stopped, Jessica's eyes just above his chin level.

"About dinner yesterday evening." Sean's voice dropped low, the timbre of it riding an electrical pulse up Jessica's spine. "I know it was interrupted and all but…thanks."

He didn't need to look at her that way. It made her feel things she'd rather not acknowledge. "It was no big—"

He held up a hand, his eyes searching hers. "No. It was a big deal. It's like you knew something was wrong and you tried to make it right. Nobody's thought about what I needed for a long time and…I appreciate that."

His expression was too full of something beyond the words he was saying, words which were already out of the bounds of any place their relationship should go. The whole moment made her stomach flutter. Jessica cleared her throat and stepped back, catching her hip against the desk, then slipped around it, making a show of organizing her files. "Not even your girlfriend?"

"What girlfriend?"

"Ashley."

"Ashley?" Sean's voice rose on the last syllable. "She

needed me more than I needed her. Not that that's a bad thing. She was going through a rough time."

Was? As in past tense? Jessica stopped shuffling papers to look up at him. "Is she okay?"

"She's okay now." Sean's face darkened, a cross between regret and maybe anger. "Though that wasn't the case a few months ago."

"You broke up?"

"What?" Confused lines creased his forehead, then melted away into a slight smile. "No. Ashley's not my girlfriend. I mean, she was, but that was a huge mistake. She's a very good friend who is married to one of my other good friends."

Jessica winced, then wished she could take the action back. The last thing a guy like him wanted was her pity.

This time, Sean didn't even try to tamp down his amusement. "It's not like that. I'm happy for both of them. They're meant to be married to each other. Trust me. Ashley and I grew up together, lost our parents together. That breeds a whole other kind of love that makes you a family but has nothing to do with marriage. She's like a sister. We were engaged briefly a long time ago, but it was a gut reaction to a bad situation. Ashley was a military police officer and was shot in the line of duty. She nearly died, and the post-traumatic stress…" He slid a stack of papers to the side. "She left the Army. Now she consults with us." Sean seemed to decide the conversation was over, dropping into her chair and turning his attention to the computer screen. "A lot of things never should have happened."

The utterance was so low Jessica knew she wasn't supposed to hear it, but there was no way to deny the words. Something was definitely up with Sean Turner, and whatever it was, it ran deeper than his failed engagement or the death of his parents.

NINE

Seriously. Why did he open his mouth around her? He should pull an old-school tough guy impersonation and stick to nods and grunts. Every time they started talking, things came out that Sean never meant to say to anyone.

If he'd been smart, he'd have kept his mouth closed and let her think he was in a relationship. It wasn't her business anyway, and that whole incident between Ashley and him was something he kept close and never talked about, especially since she was nearly killed when he made her the cipher for encoded information that took down a terror cell. If he'd played that differently, she'd have never been in danger in the first place.

She also probably wouldn't be married to Ethan—and Sean would probably be dead.

He pressed his palms into the top of the desk, shoving away that line of thought. Bottom line, Ashley had been in danger because of his actions. Now he had the chance to make it right by getting Jessica Dylan out of this new situation alive. Nothing could stand in the way of that.

Not even the fact that his heart had double-timed so loudly when she stood close to him that she was bound to have been able to hear it. That was definitely not a thing he could allow to happen. Distance was best, and he meant to keep it.

Except that his stupid mouth kept shooting off. There was something about the way she looked at him. Something that reached inside and unknotted the ropes around the locked box of his heart.

He swallowed a groan. She even had him thinking like a bad poet. If Ethan or Ashley could read his mind, they'd both get a good laugh at his expense.

Forget it. The last thing he needed to worry about was Ethan or Ashley—and especially not Jessica Dylan. This was about getting to the bottom of the craziness, protecting Jessica and stopping whatever this group's plan was. Right now, that meant wading through the data on her computer. With the administrator rights granted to him by her S-4 shop, which handled all of the computer systems for her battalion, he plugged in a portable drive and uploaded the files he needed to allow Ashley to remote in.

Slipping headphones into one ear, he pulled his laptop from his backpack and held it out to Jessica. "The data from Channing's cell is already open on the desktop. While I talk to Ashley, I want you to go through each of those photos."

She hesitated before taking the laptop, probably because of his abrupt change in demeanor. It needed to be that way, even though it cut him to see her confusion. "What am I trying to find?"

"Anyone you recognize. Anything that seems out of place. Take time with each picture and really think if any of them are familiar. I can't get over the fact they have dozens of Department of Defense photos. That's not weird, it's downright bizarre. Nobody would need something like that for personal use. I didn't see anything, but you, being closer to the situation, might get deeper." He turned back to her computer and plugged the other end of his headphones into his cell. It would have been easier to use a Bluetooth, but wireless tech was too easy to hack.

Ashley answered before the first ring even finished. "I'm already in the system."

"Good morning to you, too." Sean grinned in spite of her businesslike attitude. Ashley was never more focused than when she was solving a puzzle and, judging by the number of texts she'd sent him over the past day and a half, this was a puzzle she was diving into.

"Sorry. I'm just really, really curious about this one."

"You and me both, kiddo."

"I've been up since five, going over the files you sent. From the data, the phone was used like a burner phone, but it's not a burner. It checks out with Channing's name and personal info and everything. Thing is, it's only been used to call or text two numbers, and all of the texts are encrypted or at least in code."

"You tracked down the other two numbers?"

"Burner phones, prepaids bought with cash, impossible to trace. Ethan was able to pull some strings and get surveillance footage from one of the purchases. It was a kid, probably no more than sixteen. We'll try to track him down, but chances are high someone paid him to go in the store and buy that phone."

"Hmm." Sean sat back in the seat and rocked back and forth, watching the mouse dance across the screen as Ashley took control of the computer from her home office in Virginia. "And the pictures?"

"Far as I can tell, they're standard Department of Defense photos. But the question is how your suspect got original files. Those files aren't scans of photos. They're actual photos."

"Fakes?"

"If they are, they're good. Someone knew exactly what they were doing, down to having the same cameras used in the ID card facilities. Only other possibility is someone hacked the database, but that would be a risky hack just to get a handful of pictures."

It had to be about more than the pictures, but Sean couldn't quite figure out what. "Here's another bit for you to factor in. Channing's uniforms aren't hers." While he dragged out and fired up Jessica's laptop, using her ID card to log in, he filled Ashley in on yesterday's findings. "Military police investigations processed the room, and I'm waiting to get access to what they found, but my guy at the station says it wasn't anything out of the ordinary."

"Did Channing have a computer?"

Of course Ashley would ask that first. She'd love to get her hands on more hardware to play with. Sean grinned, and then frowned. "Not unless she has it on her. There was no tech in the room. All we've got is the phone, and they wiped it clean remotely. I doubt they know I've backed it up, so we're a step ahead."

"Okay." Ashley was disappointed and holding back a sigh. Figured. She'd just been denied her right to more gadgets to snoop around in.

The mouse on the screen jumped again, and several new windows opened, then arranged in a square.

Sean scanned each one, looking on as Ashley's second set of eyes. Encryption and coding were his specialty, but Ashley had taken it far beyond his training. He was here to back her up, to let her do her thing and read behind her on the off chance she missed something. Highly unlikely.

"You said Channing accessed the computer on Monday?"

Sean nodded before he realized she couldn't see it. "Yep. Start there."

Less than thirty seconds and two more windows passed before Ashley let out a small whoop. "Found it." She let out a low whistle. "She didn't download data. She uploaded it. And she had it buried deep. The file changed its own upload date."

"So how do you know—"

"Because I'm good. Don't ask questions that will take two hours to answer." She laughed, clearly excited to know more than him about something.

Behind Sean, Jessica shifted in her seat, and her breathing grew closer. She was watching. Who could blame her? It was fascinating to see a computer seemingly take control of itself. "What's going on?"

Sean laid a hand over the mic and turned to find Jessica leaning across the desk, closer than he'd thought. He cleared his throat, going for professional and hoping he hit it. "There's a rogue file on your computer, uploaded by Channing on Monday before the attack. We're tracking it now."

She nodded but didn't step back, just hovered, watching the screen.

Ashley drew him back into her work. "There are several files." A few more clicks and she lined several windows up across the screen. "Far left is a keystroke tracker. Anything Staff Sergeant Dylan types, they're going to log."

"Including us right now?"

"Not since I remoted in. I blocked all traffic but ours. But they likely captured her password when she logged you in. And do you see this?" The mouse wandered over to a window in the middle of the screen. "It's a back door into the system. They opened up their own entrance to

Staff Sergeant Dylan's computer. They can do anything they want, upload new software, manipulate files, delete data. They've set up camp in her system. And if they're watching right now, they're probably scrambling, trying to figure out why their door is shut."

"Stop gloating." Sean could hear it in her voice. "And reopen it when you're finished. We don't want them to know we're onto them."

"I'm not in kindergarten. I've got this." She tapped a few more keys. "There's another file I'm going to have to spend some more time with because I've not seen anything like it before, but the back door has a hacker's signature in the code. I'm going to run it against a few databases and see if we lock on to anybody who's known, maybe start from there."

"How long?"

"Hours if you're lucky. Days if you're not."

He was afraid of that. "Okay. You keep snooping and I'm going to check out the laptop, see if I can figure out what makes it worth stealing. Get back to me with any findings. And save me some of that pie."

"You won't be back for Thanksgiving. And how did you know about the pie?"

"Ethan." They said it together, then Sean hung up, picturing Ethan and Ashley with his parents around the table in their brand-new house, showing off their home for the first time. Sean wouldn't have fit in. For the first time since his own parents died, he wanted more than football and dinner with his buddies. He wanted…

What? Even he couldn't define it, but the picture of Ethan and Ashley's family Thanksgiving made his stomach raw with jealousy.

"Find anything?" Jessica's voice dragged him out of a building melancholy.

It didn't matter what he wanted. Until he beat back the dragons that ate up his sleeping thoughts, he couldn't focus on anything other than being the best soldier he could be. "Ashley's running the files on your computer against an international database of known hackers. It could be a while."

Jessica nodded and sat back down, finger flicking across the touch pad as she studied each photo carefully, her forehead wrinkled in concentration.

Sean shifted the laptop on the desk, making a show of fidgeting with it but watching Jessica instead, while she was too focused on her task to notice. Her dark hair was twisted back in a knot according to regulations, but it waved where it wasn't pulled tight enough. The set of her jaw said she was oblivious to his scrutiny, totally absorbed in her search.

She was beautiful. No man could deny that. Still, there was something else about her... The way she'd fried her precious chicken last night because she knew he needed it. The way she stressed over the women who were supposed to be at her Bible study, but still rearranged her plans to make sure they stayed safe. The fact she'd given up an afternoon to reassure a young wife over something as simple as a trip to the ID card facility. She thought of others over herself, and that was something that doubled her attractiveness. Something Sean hadn't noticed about another woman since he and Ashley had parted ways. Maybe not even then. As much as Ashley was his best friend, loving her had become a habit, a given that they would get married. Without passion, it was purely platonic, a mistaken effort to help her restore a life spinning out of control, a decision made out of fear on both of their behalf.

But Jessica Dylan? There was something there he couldn't quite deny, no matter how badly he wanted to.

As if she read his thoughts, her head jerked up. But instead of noticing him, she shoved his laptop forward, hand trembling slightly. "I know this soldier."

Sean reached for the machine. "Who is it?"

"Specialist Andrew Murphy. Our dead soldier."

TEN

"You're sure that's your casualty." Sean dropped everything he was doing, sliding her laptop aside to pull his closer.

Jessica stared at the photo on the screen. Specialist Murphy was a cutup, one who'd barely made it overseas without the first sergeant tearing him to pieces for complete insubordination. There were moments when half the battalion wondered how the kid ever made it out of basic with his utter lack of seriousness. Even in this, what appeared to be an ID card photo, his smirk was clearly in evidence.

"It's him." She pushed away from the desk, working hard to keep the shock from coming through in her voice. "That's Andrew Murphy."

"Did he know Specialist Channing? Were they friends?" Sean stared at the screen as though he was trying to memorize the image. As though he thought the answers would pop up in the background.

Jessica shook her head. "Not to my knowledge, at least not here at Campbell. He deployed with the rest of the battalion. Channing just got here as a replacement last week. We can pull their records and see if they were ever stationed together before."

"Let's do that. And as soon as we get an ID on our guy at the hospital, we'll pull his records, too. Somewhere, there's a link between the three of them that may give us some answers. How did Murphy die?"

"Stepped on an improvised explosive device while on patrol."

Sean slumped. "He never knew what hit him."

"Not exactly. He survived the blast, but barely. He had a reaction during his blood transfusion and his body was too broken to fight it off." In her job as a medic, Jessica had seen more than one soldier chewed up by an IED. Almost always there was amputation involved and, with enough charge, there could be nothing at all identifiable. Sometimes, the entire contents of her aid bag weren't enough. The sights and sounds and smells of a post-IED incident had her bolting up gasping for air some nights, feeling as if she could have done more.

"You okay?"

Jessica lifted her head to find Sean watching her with that look he had, as if he'd managed to get into her head and read her mind. "I'm fine. Just…remembering."

He acted as if he was going to say something, but then turned his attention back to his laptop instead.

It took all of her willpower not to call him out on what he'd almost said. Maybe he knew of a way to make the visions go away. She'd give anything for a way to turn off the movies that intruded on her sleep.

Instead, Sean studied the photo, then slid the laptop to the side. "Okay, let's run through this. Like we said earlier, it could be some weird dating site that uses Defense photos."

"That would be too weird to be for real."

"True, but I'm trying to think outside the box." Sean rocked back in the chair. "Most soldiers I know really aren't fond of mixing their Army lives with their social lives. Well, unless they're hoping the uniform will get them some mileage with a woman."

"There's that. But a dating site based on your service? That's sort of abuse of the uniform, at least to me." Curiosity wanted to ask if Sean had ever used whatever his considerable credentials had to be to get "mileage," but she kept her mouth shut. What he did in his off time was none of her business, but she couldn't deny feeling disappointed in him if he ever had. Somehow, he didn't seem the type, and she fervently hoped she was right.

"So we recognize two of the photos, Murphy and your unwelcome guest from yesterday. I didn't see Channing's photo in there last night, but then again, I only flipped through them." Sean sat forward and clasped his hands on the desk. "Have you been through them all? Seen if there are more people you know?"

Jessica shook her head. The sight of Murphy's face staring up at her had stopped everything. "I've studied about a dozen. There's probably two times that many left for me to check out."

"But none of the others so far were soldiers in your unit or even people that you recognized?"

"No, but I wasn't here very long before the brigade left. That's how I drew Rear D. Not enough time since my last deployment. I knew a lot of people in passing, but not well. Murphy stood out because he was always riding the line right on the edge of trouble."

Sean ran his thumb along the side of his index finger, thinking. "Two laptops stolen from each unit. One of yours stolen, and an attempt to steal this one. Terrorist chatter spiked each time. A keystroke tracker and a back door on your desktop. Two people willing to kill you rather than let you reveal what they're doing, even though other witnesses saw them. A soldier whose gear is hers, but her clothing isn't. Another soldier who tries to attack you, then breaks into your house. And a dead soldier with no apparent link other than this picture on Channing's phone." Sean sat back and threw his hands in the air. "I've got nothing."

"Are we sure they're all related?"

"No. But they all link back to that phone and Specialist Channing, who hasn't been seen since Monday. What do you know about her?"

"Nothing other than what's in her file. This is her second duty station, her first deployment. She's been in a couple of years and she just got here, going over as a replacement in the unit. Channing grew up a foster kid with no family. Like I said, I only know that because she listed her Designated Person on her DD-93 as a friend from basic training."

"You've called the friend?"

"Battalion did. Friend hasn't heard from her in a couple of months. Just said Channing is a good soldier who was excited about finally going overseas to see some action." Quite a few young soldiers who weren't battle tested thought war was excitement and romance, the stuff of movies and video games. They learned fast that real life didn't have a rewind or a reset.

Jessica shook off a shudder, trying to focus on the problem at hand instead of the trauma she'd seen in the past.

If Sean thought this whole thing made a mess in his brain, Jessica had no way to describe the chaos in hers. He was likely used to twists in investigations. For her part, she had no experience whatsoever in riddles like this one. Bullet wounds, she could patch. Shrapnel, she could stop the bleeding. Computers and cell phones and random events? There wasn't any logic to any of this, nothing she could put her hands on and fix. It made her head pound harder than the dull ache she'd had for days.

Sean exhaled loudly, then snapped his fingers and sat straighter. "You said there's a Casualty Assistance Officer with Murphy's family?"

"With his great-aunt in Iowa." Jessica sat up in her chair and leaned forward, eager to get some momentum and end this nightmare that had clawed itself into her daylight. "You have an idea?"

"We want to try to find any link between Channing and Murphy. Forward that photo and one of Channing to whoever the officer is. I'll set up a list of questions for him to gently ask the aunt, take his time, work them in. She's grieving and we don't want to push too hard, especially if Murphy is innocent, which he could be. Being a photo on someone's cell phone doesn't constitute a criminal act."

Jessica nodded and pushed up out of the chair to find the commander and identify the Casualty Assistance Officer. "Anything else?"

Sean pulled in a deep breath and started to speak, but his phone vibrated on the desk. He glanced at the screen, then at Jessica, and picked it up. "Turner." His jaw set tight and he nodded, listening. "Shoot the file to my email. I'll be there within the hour." He hung up without saying another word and stood, shoving the phone into his pocket. "I've been cleared to talk to the man from your house."

Jessica stood, too. "I'm going with you." She wanted to look that man in the eye and ask him why. Why did he want her dead?

"No." Sean's denial held the weight of cement, the gravity so heavy it wouldn't even let her fill her lungs.

"I'm not putting you in a room with him until I know who's behind this and what they're capable of."

"But—" He couldn't deny her the opportunity to face the man who'd tried to kill her.

"No." Sean rounded the desk and looked down at her, the ghost of his earlier emotion shadowing his face and softening the lines around his mouth. "I need you safe." He pressed a kiss to her forehead and lingered there for a second.

His touch sent a twinge down her spine, like electricity from a lightning bolt, but she wasn't going to let that distract her. She stepped back, putting as much distance between them as she could in the small space. She could be attracted to him all she wanted, but she wasn't going to let momentary emotions knock her off course. "Half an hour ago, you didn't think this very office was safe. You thought I needed you hounding my steps everywhere I go. Which is it? You can't have it both ways." It wasn't that she needed him to take care of her, but she'd use any leverage she could to force him to take her along. The man lying in that hospital bed was after her, and she wasn't about to be left out of the loop now. "You seemed to think I'm only safe when you're around, remember?"

The slight flare of his nostrils told Jessica she'd hit her mark. Either that or he didn't like her pulling away from him. He tightened his jaw and looked over her head, likely trying to gather his composure. He acquiesced with a loud sigh, snatching her jacket from the back of her chair and holding it out to her. "Fine. Let's go. But you're not stepping foot into that room unless I give you the okay."

She smirked at his back as he walked out the door ahead of her. That was fine. She'd managed to change his mind once. She shouldn't have any problem doing it again.

We'd like to send you two free books from the series you are enjoying now. Your two books have a combined cover price of over $10, but are yours to keep absolutely FREE! We'll even send you two wonderful surprise gifts. You can't lose!

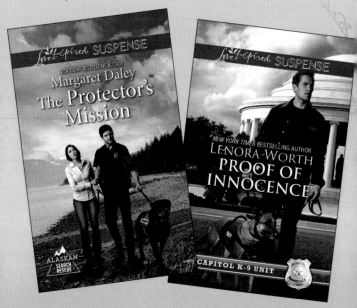

Each of your FREE books is filled with joy, faith and traditional values a and women open their hearts to each other and join together on a spirit journey.

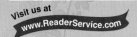

GET 2 FREE BOOKS!

HURRY!
Return this card today to get 2 FREE Books and 2 FREE Bonus Gifts!

▼ DETACH AND MAIL CARD TODAY! ▼

YES! Please send me the **2 FREE books** and **2 FREE gifts** for which I qualify. I understand that I am under no obligation to purchase anything further, as explained on the back of this card.

```
PLACE
FREE GIFTS
SEAL HERE
```

❏ I prefer the regular-print edition
153/353 IDL GHP6

❏ I prefer the larger-print edition
107/307 IDL GHUJ

FIRST NAME

LAST NAME

ADDRESS

APT.#

CITY

STATE/PROV.

ZIP/POSTAL CODE

SLI-N15-IV15

READER SERVICE—Here's how it works:

* * *

Sean walked up the hallway of the small hospital in Clarksville, still mentally kicking himself twenty minutes after leaving Jessica's office. Why had he kissed her, even on the forehead? There was absolutely nothing professional about that. Something about her undid his reserve and kept him from thinking straight. From now on, he had to stay six feet away from her at all times. Six full feet. Touching her was definitely off-limits from here on out. Just the thought of his impetuous stupidity made his neck burn. There was no telling what she was thinking about him right now, and it would be a wonder if he wasn't sitting in sensitivity training by this afternoon.

Jessica hadn't given him a clue to her thoughts, either. She'd been silent the entire ride, watching the trees fly by along the highway. He couldn't blame her. If he was the one standing in her shoes, he wouldn't talk to him, either.

Stepping into the elevator, he tried to breathe through his mouth. All hospitals were interchangeable, at least when it came to his nose. The antiseptic smell of medicine and floor cleaner gave off a scent more like death than healing. It all but choked him. Too much like sitting at Ashley's bedside when infection from a bullet wound nearly took her. Too much like his own recovery, and the concern he'd lose his arm, or worse, his mind. His pulse spiked. He swallowed the visions and balled his fists to keep from grabbing on to the rail along the wall.

"I'd still like to go in with you when you question him."

Jessica pulled him out of his own mind, and the distraction was more than welcome, even if it led to a heated discussion. "We went over this. You get to come because you promised to stay out of sight. If he sees you, I don't know what he'll do. We have no idea who—"

"And if he sees me, he may talk."

Sean wanted to take her by the shoulders and make her look at him. And he would, too—if he wasn't afraid to touch her. "No."

"But—"

"You step back and you stay quiet." He infused all of his authority into the words, and they grated harsh against his ears. Although he hated to do it, he was in charge and that was the one thing she couldn't argue with.

Her jaw tightened as the muscle at the corner of her eye twitched. She straightened her posture. "Understood, *Staff Sergeant*." She shifted, putting extra inches between them.

With that action, Sean lost something with her he might never get back. Camaraderie. Trust. The beginning of whatever insisted on pulsing between them.

All for the better. He had to maintain focus if he had any chance of healing himself. Rather than strengthening his walls, everything about her tried to tear them down.

A uniformed officer stood outside the door to the hospital room, while a man in civilian clothes spoke to a nurse nearby. Sean could read the training by the way he stood. A detective.

Sean waited for the nurse to walk away before holding out his hand. "Staff Sergeant Sean Turner." He turned toward Jessica, who had her focus firmly locked on the detective. "Staff Sergeant Dylan."

"Detective Ken Altman." The man stepped forward and pulled his hand from the pocket of his black jacket to shake Sean's, then Jessica's. He paused. "This guy broke into your house?"

She nodded but didn't speak, probably shoving Sean's directive back in his face.

Altman turned to Sean. "I don't understand all you've got going on here, but somebody high up wants this guy secure. I'm going to need to see some ID before you can go in."

Sean understood, even felt relief at the seriousness with which local law enforcement was handling this. The last thing he needed was their one solid suspect escaping. He pulled his military ID from his wallet and handed it over. "What have you gotten out of him?"

"Not a word." The detective scanned Sean's ID and handed it back. "He hasn't spoken, not to anyone. He just stares at us. Makes me wonder if he can speak English."

"He lawyered up?"

"No. When I say *not a word*, I literally mean not one word."

"He's more afraid of someone else than he is of us."

Detective Altman tapped the side of his nose. "You got it. What are you thinking?"

"I'm still putting pieces together." While he wanted to cooperate, Sean held his information close. If the military felt the situation merited his unit's involvement, it meant no one outside could be trusted, no matter what badge they carried. It was only when necessary that others were informed, as with the instance when the FBI hostage rescue team had been called in for him.

It couldn't get that far this time.

"Maybe he'll talk to you." Detective Altman stepped aside. "Want me to come with you?"

"Let me go alone. Maybe seeing me will spook him."

Altman snorted. "It oughtta. You're the reason he's in here in the first place."

Sean didn't reply. He simply stepped around the officer at the door and pushed through without a glance at Jessica. She would take him down with a glare.

It took a moment for his eyes to adjust to the small interior room. Their suspect lay on the bed with his eyes closed, but as Sean drew nearer, he opened them. While the man tried to appear relaxed, the lines around his mouth tightened, tension stiffening his neck. His uninjured arm lay by his side, a handcuff firmly attaching him to the rail.

Sean didn't give an inch. It was clear the guy remembered him. The question was would he talk.

"Found something interesting today." Sean pulled Channing's phone from his pocket and flipped it over in his hands. He watched carefully, searching for signs of recognition, but there were none. The guy was younger than he'd first thought, no more than twenty-two, and if he knew anything about the former contents of the phone, he was skilled at schooling his reaction.

Okay, let him play mute. There were plenty of ways to bluff information out of him. "Found your picture on the cell phone of a suspected terrorist. Care to explain before I let Homeland take a shot at federal charges?"

No fear. Only a smirk laced with arrogance quirked their suspect's lip. Whoever this kid was, he thought he could get away with his scheme.

Or he didn't care.

Time to raise the stakes. Sliding the chair closer, Sean pocketed Channing's phone and retrieved his own. He scrolled through it, letting the quiet weigh heavy. From experience, the brain could only take so much silence before the need to fill it became overwhelming, before the mind spun out of control imagining scenarios far worse than real life could ever provide.

Except for those rare times when real life exceeded every conceivable nightmare.

Sean fought a grimace and endured the silence for

ten long minutes, staring at nothing on his phone as he waited for his subject to crack.

The man on the bed stared at the ceiling, occasionally yawning.

But the silence told Sean more than words ever could, and the information it fed him chilled his blood more than any threat.

This kid was trained and trained well. Getting him to crack would take more than Sean's skill and likely more than they could legally throw at him. Training like that only came in camps that drew die-hard recruits with a hard-core hatred of America.

Camps that indicated this might be larger than he'd contemplated.

Sean flipped to the file the detective had emailed and stared at the words on the screen, choosing his strategy carefully. "I've got a buddy who used to be in Special Forces. He tells the story about this warlord they were searching for in Afghanistan. He'd fired up this new terror cell and it was on track to outpace al-Qaeda. Everybody was after this guy, but he never left a trace. He was a ghost. And then…they grabbed him in a cave near the Pakistani border.

"Know how they found him?" Sean blew up the file on the screen, reading through the information, letting the pause stretch. "Jelly beans." He chuckled, still genuinely amused by Tate's story. "Guy had this crazy addiction to American jelly beans. He'd order them off the internet and have one of his men ferry them in. Once our guys figured out the source, all they had to do was follow the candy. Weaknesses can get us." Boy, did he know that.

"There's another guy." Sean rested his elbows on his knees, staring at his mark as he drew out the story. "Had an affinity for something a little harder than jelly beans. Vodka, was it?" He made a show of glancing at the phone, watching the man out of his peripheral vision.

One eyebrow twitched, and the muscles in his jaw tightened.

There it was. Sean had the kid right where he wanted him. "Seems that guy forgot that when you fake an ID at nineteen and the cops catch you, they fingerprint you and put you into the system. Six years was a long time ago, so maybe the guy forgot. Or maybe he was cocky enough to think he'd never get caught again. What do you think, Kyle Randall?"

Randall's eyes narrowed, filled with the kind of malice Sean had only seen one other time in his life. It was the kind of hatred that came from a desperate person who knew time was short. The kind of hatred that would do anything to save itself.

Sean fought to keep his heart rate level. His nightmares couldn't invade this moment. Too much was at stake. He swallowed hard, willing down a fear that would turn the tables before he got the answers he sought.

Needing a minute to pull himself together, he stood and paced to the door, looking out the small window to reassure himself that Jessica was safe, that backup was outside. When he saw Altman and Jessica talking in the hall, he steeled himself and turned back to Kyle Randall, who was watching with an expression that said he knew he was about to fall prey to the dogs.

"Right now, Kyle, we've got several agencies checking into your background, because we suspect you're into something big. If I were going to guess, I'd say we're going to find a passport. And on that passport, we're going to find you've made some extended trips overseas. And when we find those trips, we're going to turn you over to another agency that won't be as nice as I will be if you start talking right now."

Sean stepped closer, staying just out of arm's reach. "To me, you're the small potato that can point me to the whole field. To Homeland, you're a terrorist who tried twice to attack a female noncommissioned officer. You'll like my deal better than theirs."

Randall stared at Sean a long time before he sniffed and sank against the pillow. "Can you find out when they're serving lunch?" He stared at the ceiling, smirk firmly in place.

Sean didn't flinch. The kid had definitely been trained well. He wasn't afraid of one thing Sean threw at him. Deciding to give it a rest for the moment so Randall had plenty of time to think, Sean turned and walked for the door. His fingers brushed the handle as Kyle Randall spoke again.

"The fact is, you can't stop anything. And you got lucky saving Ashley Kincaid."

Sean didn't move, although he wanted to drive a fist into Randall's mouth. *How did this guy know he'd saved Ashley and she'd married Ethan Kincaid?*

"We went after Staff Sergeant Dylan at first because she'd seen us. She could identify our people. But then you got involved and stepped in as her protector. And you need to know this…" Randall's voice dropped low, hard. "They'll take her. They'll torture her. And you can't do a thing to stop it."

ELEVEN

Clasping her fingers behind her back, Jessica eyed the door to the hospital room. She should be in there. And if Detective Altman wasn't standing guard with the other police officer, she'd have charged through and made her presence known. She had a right to know why the man in custody thought she was better off dead. In fact, her right to know was greater than Sean's.

She pushed air out through teeth clenched so tight her jaw ached. He'd actually pulled rank on her. Up until that moment, they'd been in this together, but that single command put her squarely in her place. He was in charge and she was merely along for the ride because his orders were to watch out for her. Nothing more.

It shouldn't hurt, but it did.

She laced her fingers tighter together. Well, he'd made his feelings clear, so she wouldn't make the mistake of letting hers get drawn in by him again.

The door to the room eased open, pulling Altman and his officer to attention.

Jessica straightened as Sean stepped out the door and pulled it shut carefully behind him.

Her anger evaporated. Something was wrong. Very wrong. Sean Turner was always in control, but in this moment that control was calculated, riding the edge of a razor. Whatever had happened in that room, it hadn't gone the way he wanted.

He flicked a glance at her, his jaw set tight, then found Detective Altman and jerked his chin up the hall. "Over here." Sean stalked away without checking to see if anyone followed, his shoulders an unbreakable line.

Jessica fell into step behind the detective, careful to keep her footfalls nearly silent. She hadn't been invited to this little sidebar, but there was no way Sean was keeping her out of the loop any longer.

Halfway to the elevators, Sean whipped around and fired a look at Detective Altman that forced the older man to take a step back. "Did you tell Randall I was coming? Mention my name? Tell him anything about me?" Anger colored the words red and hot.

Altman shook his head but, to his credit, didn't seem fazed by Sean's fury. "Not a word." He looked back at the officer by the door. "And I was the only one who knew."

"He had no way of knowing anything about me?" Sean's words were hard, demanding answers.

Jessica stepped around Detective Altman. Sean had never once seemed rattled, but this… This anger wasn't just anger. There was something else behind it, something she'd glimpsed in smaller doses before. "What happened?"

He seemed to see her for the first time, and it did something to his demeanor, something that couldn't quite be explained but that relaxed his posture the slightest bit.

Jessica braced for him to issue another directive.

Instead, he seemed to be trying to memorize her face before he turned back to the detective, who watched the two of them with interest. "He confessed to coming after Staff Sergeant Dylan. And I want everything you have on him as soon as you get it. Everything, even if it seems completely insignificant to you." He turned and stalked toward the elevators.

Jessica opened her mouth and closed it, turning to the detective. The female in her wanted to apologize for Sean's behavior, but the soldier kept her mouth shut. "We'll be in touch. Thank you."

She practically had to run to catch Sean, who'd apparently decided the elevator was too slow and was pushing open the door for the stairs. She grabbed his arm as he stepped through, her anger resurging, voice sharp. "Hey." She stepped aside to let the door shut behind her but kept her hand on his forearm. "What is going on?"

His muscles were steely beneath her fingers. Sean worked his jaw back and forth, not turning toward her, keeping his focus on the corner at the turn of the stairs.

"Talk to me." Jessica relaxed her grip but didn't let go. "You're not acting like yourself."

Sean exhaled and his muscles relaxed, but he still didn't look at her. "The guy isn't talking."

This was what had him so spun up? "He's not talking at all? That's the problem? But you said he confessed."

He finally met her gaze, but only for a second. "He's almost totally mute. But the detective emailed me his file when we were on the way over. His name's Kyle Randall. He has a record for making a very passable fake ID when he was underage and buying alcohol. His fingerprints caught up to him."

"Wait. His fingerprints caught up to him? For a crime? There's nothing to identify him as a soldier?"

He'd wondered if she'd catch that. "No. The guy isn't a soldier."

That was impossible. This made no sense. "But he

was in uniform at the ID card facility. What was he doing there?"

"I don't know. The question I want answered is was he there watching you? Or was he there working on a bigger plot? If he was following you, why would he need a uniform? Civilians go into the ID card facility all of the time. Even contractors have to have a common access card issued." He shrugged, finally glancing at her, but turning away just as fast. "The more I know, the less I understand." He pulled his hand from her arm and started down the stairs again, taking them as fast as he could without falling on his face. "I need to get you back to safety and then I need to get a secure message out to Ethan. Fast."

Jessica followed, her boots echoing with his in a melody against the walls of the stairwell. "What are you not telling me?"

He stopped so abruptly she almost mowed him down. When he turned to face her, they were eye to eye on the stairs. He scanned her face, searching for something. "Kyle Randall and his people know about me."

"We already knew that. They sent a message to you in your email. And your name tape is on your jacket." Sean turned to walk down the stairs, but she grabbed his bicep. "Would you stop charging around like a mad dog and tell me something?"

He stopped and turned back, finally locking eyes with her. He studied her, everything else falling away as he searched her face. "It changes everything."

"How?"

"They knew about Ashley, and he threatened..." He kept studying her face. Finally, he slipped his arm from her grasp and reached for her hand, holding it tight in cold fingers. "There are some things you don't know.

Things that happened to Ashley. Things about why I was in Afghanistan. And maybe it's time—"

Before he could finish, her phone rang.

She ignored it vibrating in her chest pocket. The connection between them was too important, too raw. It tugged at her heart and swirled in her stomach. Her voice dropped lower. "What is it?"

He tipped his head toward her, dropping her hand. "Answer that. It could be important."

"Or it could be nothing."

He took a step backward down the stairs, opening the space between them and letting it fill with empty air.

Jessica tried not to shiver at the sudden chill as she drew the phone from her pocket and answered it, her free hand reaching for Sean's arm. "Captain Alexander?"

"Staff Sergeant Dylan, we have a problem."

Her fingers tightened on the phone. Surely she wasn't about to get yelled at for leaving the office at lunch? That seemed a petty complaint in the midst of everything else. "What kind of problem, sir?"

"I just got a call from a sheriff in Lincoln County, Colorado. They found a body out there, a Jane Doe." The captain stopped talking, as if he couldn't quite believe what he was about to say. "Well, they thought it was a Jane Doe until they got the DNA back and traced her to our battalion. Dylan, their dead body is Specialist Lindsay Channing."

"I'm going for a run. Alone." Jessica pushed the side door to her house open and threw her bag down by a wooden bench without stopping.

Sean shut the door behind him, weighing his next words carefully. That call from her commander had him rattled, too, and that was the precise reason he wouldn't let her out of this house without an escort. Details of the horrors of Channing's death only confirmed that Randall's threats weren't empty. These people would do exactly as they said—take Jessica and torture her.

Sean wouldn't let that happen, for reasons he wasn't even fully ready to admit even to himself. He steeled himself and called after her as she retreated up the hallway. "You're not going out alone. Not after what we've learned today."

Her booted feet thunked to a halt at the foot of the stairs, but she didn't turn around. Instead, she tilted her head toward the sky.

Was she praying?

Finally, her posture slumped. "Fine. But I'm going upstairs. Alone. I need to be alone." She turned the corner and vanished, her footfalls growing more muted as she ascended the stairs.

Sean stared after her a long time. That was almost too easy. He'd been prepared for an argument, a showdown. Her acquiescence was a surprise. Maybe, like him, she was too overwhelmed to fight about the small stuff anymore.

Or she was going to sneak out the back window and climb down a hidden trellis.

Wrapping his fingers tighter around the strap of his backpack, he headed for the couch and settled the bag on the table, then dropped onto the cushions. He couldn't fault her for needing some time to herself. The way his brain was spinning, the quiet would do him good, as well. Somehow, he had to find a way to put together everything that was happening. Somewhere, there was an answer to who was doing this—and why. If he could just get an anchor dug in, he could build the rest of the case around it. The problem was, he had no idea where to start. Might as well drag his laptop back out and go through the data from Channing's cell phone. Again.

He leaned forward to pull his backpack across the coffee table, but a flash of light outside caught his eye. The red sports car Channing and her partner had escaped in slowed to a stop in front of the house and sat idling.

Pulse quickening, Sean eased his backpack closer and unzipped the front pocket, slipping his Sig from the holster tucked inside. It was doubtful the occupants of the car could see into the house, but he kept his movements small and easy, trying to watch the goings-on without being seen.

No one exited the car. No motion showed through the tinted windows. It was a silent standoff, one that Sean couldn't get a read on. Were they merely watching, or were they waiting to let loose a barrage of gunfire? Was there a car bomb in the vehicle, waiting to unleash enough force to level the house and anyone inside? The uncertainty made Sean want to charge out the front door and confront whoever was in the vehicle head-on.

But he didn't dare. Going out without cover would make him a wide-open target. He reached for his hip pocket to pull out his cell phone and call Tate in the guest room, trying to avoid any noise or movement that would set off the driver of the sports car. Just as his fingers brushed the case, the car squealed away from the curb and took off down the street.

Sean was up and out the front door but the car had disappeared around the next block. He pounded his fist against his thigh. He ought to jump in his car and follow them, but that would leave Jessica alone upstairs with Tate sound asleep in the guest room. If this was some sort of setup, his giving chase was exactly what they wanted.

That whole incident crawled down his spine. The

driver of that car had wanted to be seen. There was no other reason for it. The question was why.

Keeping his weapon close to avoid anyone on the street noticing it, Sean backed toward the front door, scanning the trees and shrubs in nearby yards, searching for any sign of a hidden antagonist.

The street was silent in the middle of the day with kids in school and adults at work. Outside of a slight breeze, nothing stirred. But the stillness didn't curb Sean's apprehension. The quiet only served to heighten his senses. Something wasn't right.

One quick look around the house, just to be sure, then he'd go back inside and check every single window and door personally. Until he did that, there would be no relaxing.

Keeping the open front door in sight, he tried to look casual, strolling to the side yard for a peek. The small grassy area by the porch was silent, the cars in the driveway seemingly untouched.

Surely they wouldn't try the same window Kyle Randall had used. Sean passed the front of the house again, scanning the windows and porch roof, seeing nothing. The side yard was empty, the windows tightly closed.

If the driver of that car had wanted him paranoid, he or she had succeeded. It felt as though eyes watched him from every house on the street as he climbed the steps and went back in the front door, pulling it shut and twisting the dead bolt behind him. From the back of the house came the slight hum of water running through the pipes. Otherwise, there was nothing. He'd check the backyard and let that be the end of it.

Though he doubted he'd even catch his usual short sleep tonight, wondering if that sports car idled somewhere on the street, watching.

Careful to keep his footsteps light so as not to disturb Tate, Sean eased open the door to the laundry room, trying to hear over the sound of water running in Jessica's upstairs bathroom. As his hand touched the knob to the door that led to the covered porch, a scraping sound came from outside and overhead. It stopped, then started again, louder, a heavy thud punctuating the soft noise.

Adrenaline surging, Sean pressed close to the wall and peeked through the thin curtains on a small window. No movement on the porch, which meant someone had to be on the porch roof.

The very roof that ran under Jessica's bedroom window.

Whoever was up there must have assumed Sean had taken the bait and followed the sports car up the block, leaving only a sleeping Tate to guard Jessica—if they even realized Tate was in the house.

Sean tightened his grip on his pistol and twisted the doorknob. There was no time to wake Tate and no time to run upstairs. He was on his own. If he hesitated any longer, their intruder would be inside Jessica's room before Sean could get to her and save her.

Weapon at the ready, he slipped out the door and onto the covered porch. Staying close to the wall, Sean scanned the yard for anyone who might be waiting in the silence, desperately hoping whoever was on the roof of the porch was acting alone. It was unlikely. With the red sports car in play, this was no one-man show.

There was no movement. Sean waited as long as he dared before he eased away from the house, focus turned upward to the low roof of the porch that ran halfway around the back of the house before wrapping around to the front.

Dressed in gray with a cap pulled low over his face, a

man crouched low on the gentle slope of the roof, kneeling in front of the window past Jessica's, the one that led into Angie's room.

Sean's jaw tightened. Somehow, the guy knew the layout of the house and knew Angie wouldn't be home. He wasn't going straight into Jessica's room, which could get him caught. He was aiming for the room next to hers, trying to gain entrance to the house before going after Jessica.

And he had the guts to do it in broad daylight, when he knew their guard would be down. The realization ran acid into Sean's gut and chilled his fingers. These guys were serious—and desperate.

Leveling his weapon, Sean took aim and made sure he had his target sighted before calling out. "Back away from the window."

The figure froze, shoulders a hard line beneath his gray jacket. His chin lifted slightly, but he didn't turn toward Sean.

"I said back away." Sean drove all of his authority into the words, hoping Tate wouldn't hear and come running into danger. Hoping even more that Jessica wouldn't turn off the shower and open her window to investigate.

The intruder had to back down or else Sean would be forced to fire. At this range, with the ancient siding on the house, the bullet would likely penetrate the walls, and he couldn't risk hitting Jessica.

"Now." Sean held his hand steady, even though his insides quaked. If the man called his bluff and dove through that window, Jessica would be dead before Sean could get up the stairs.

The movement was imperceptible at first, but the intruder lifted his hands, tugging his hat lower over his face as he did.

Sean wanted to relax in relief, but he didn't dare. This was far from over. He swept the porch, looking for a way off the nearly flat roof. The guy must have come up from the side. Tate had padlocked the gate leading to the side yard to prevent this very thing, but it hadn't kept their uninvited guest from scaling the roof.

If he could kick himself right now, he would. How could he have missed the obvious entry point?

It didn't matter now. He could worry about it all after he had the man in custody. "You should be able to climb down to the railing and slide off. Get moving."

Sean kept his weapon steady as the man edged passed Jessica's window along the roof toward the center of the porch. Just before he reached the point Sean had indicated, the intruder stood and ran for the corner of the house.

Sean's finger went for the trigger, hesitating. He could blast through the wall and hit Jessica on the other side. Before he could sight in again, the man disappeared around the corner.

Running for the gate, Sean slid to a stop on the grass and pounded his palm against the padlocked entry as tires squealed from the other side.

He drove the side of his fist against the wood, relishing the pain that jolted up his arm. He'd blown it in the clinch. Hesitated when he should have fired. Missed the obvious plan and failed to call Tate in for backup.

If Jessica had been taken, it would have been all his fault.

TWELVE

Jessica dragged her knife through a green pepper, her face screwed up in that look she had when she was so deep in thought that the rest of the world fell away. She was oblivious to the danger that had come so close to her only half an hour earlier. Sean and Tate had felt it better to not rock her fragile security further, but they'd redoubled their efforts to protect the house. If the bad guys were getting bold enough to try a midday grab, there was no telling what their next step would be.

From outside, the sounds of a push mower rose and fell faintly, adding a low hum to the scene. The familiar sound calmed Sean's nerves, reminding him of warm summer afternoons mowing the grass while his parents worked in the small garden on their land. Right now, he chose to focus on those good memories.

Cliff diving into the current situation could kill him.

Sean stood in the kitchen door, watching Jessica work, the weight of the afternoon's events heavy on his shoulders. It was all he could do not to cross the room and pull her close, to reassure himself that his lapse in security hadn't cost her everything.

He had to relax, had to let the afternoon go. If he didn't,

she'd feel the tension pouring off him. She was astute enough to realize something was wrong.

Maybe even astute enough to realize he was afraid for her, not because she was his responsibility, but because he was feeling way too much for a woman he'd only just met.

Hopefully, she'd attribute his stress to their latest intel. So much was happening, and none of it made sense. The conversation with their suspect at the hospital rattled him more than he cared to admit. If Kyle Randall knew who Ashley was, there might be unfinished business Sean didn't even want to consider.

Sean had passed the message through to Ethan and Ashley, and they'd moved from their home to safety at the unit's main headquarters, but it didn't give Sean any peace.

Ethan, either. He'd tried to pull Sean off the op and shove him into hiding as well, but that wasn't going to happen. Sean had vowed to protect Jessica, but he couldn't put her into hiding, not without tipping their hand to the enemy. He had to see this through so he could finally put the past behind him. No more nightmares. Success was the only way to slay them. Outside of keeping Jessica alive, he didn't know how to define success in a case like this.

"Colorado." Across the kitchen, Jessica reached for another pepper, slicing it in half mechanically. "Why in the world would Channing be in Colorado?"

There it was. The other piece of information that seemed to have no place. The badly burned body of Specialist Lindsay Channing had been located in a remote area not far from Fort Carson, a single gunshot to the back of the head the preliminary cause of death. Sean caught a memory. "Wasn't Carson her duty station before she came here?"

"Yeah. But why go back there?"

"She could know someone there who agreed to hide her. She might have hooked up with whoever is behind all of this there. It's likely she trusted someone in that area, or she wouldn't have gone."

"She trusted them, and they murdered her." The knife wavered in Jessica's hand and she set it to the side, clenching and unclenching her fingers.

More than anything, Sean wanted to close the space between them and pull her close. Channing might be part of the attempts to harm Jessica, but no one deserved murder, and Jessica was feeling the pain. "There's nothing you could have done."

Jessica leaned against her hands on the counter, still not looking at Sean. "If we'd caught her here, maybe—"

"They'd have killed her here all the same." He was certain of that, especially after the attempt to breach the house this afternoon. "Apparently, she was a loose end."

"You're right." Jessica picked up her knife again and pulled another green pepper toward her, silent for long moments as the hum of the lawn mower rose and fell. "Tell me again why Tate's mowing my dead grass in November?"

Because they'd decided to let their adversaries know Sean wasn't the only one watching the house. It put Tate outside, visible but not recognizable, a subtle message to anyone watching. But he couldn't tell Jessica that without raising questions.

Sean forced a smile to tilt the corner of his lips and chose to play the game. If she wanted to take a step away from the chaos, he'd gladly lead her. There would be plenty of time to think when night fell. "He says it helps his brain focus."

Jessica arched an eyebrow but didn't pull her attention from her work. "But it's November. Nosy Major Neighbor is liable to call my father and tell him about all of the strange goings-on at the Dylan house today."

Not all of them. "Count your blessings. Tate used to use one of those manual push mowers back when he owned a B and B. Him huffing and puffing that thing around your huge backyard would draw a whole lot more attention."

"I tried that once. Thought I'd be all environmentally conscious. I returned it so fast…"

"Why's that?" Not that it mattered, but the distraction was welcome. And watching her nose scrunch with disgust was an even nicer diversion.

"Because my yard really is huge. And Tate must have lived in the Arctic. I almost sweat myself to death on a Tennessee July afternoon. Had to come in and lie on the bathroom tiles to get my body temp to drop."

Sean chuckled at her independent streak. "You're smarter than that. Didn't you pay attention during hot weather training?"

"Like you do everything exactly by the book. Yes, I paid attention. I just didn't apply my knowledge to the civilian side of my life." She flicked him a rueful glance. "I understand the weather is cooler, but I don't understand why your friend is out there right now, probably killing my grass."

Well, the conversation hadn't totally wiped that tension from her face, but it had lightened the heaviness in the room. He should have told her everything about why it mattered if the bad guys knew who he was, but he wasn't ready to burden her. She'd worry, feel pity, step up and try to protect him. That was the last thing he needed.

Even though he couldn't deny her presence was something he wanted. Somehow he knew, if she touched him, looked at him just the right way, he'd spill it all. She was safe in a way no one had ever been, not even Ashley.

He needed her, and that made her dangerous. Sean shoved his hands in his pockets, trying to keep them from taking on a life of their own by reaching out to her. That was the last thing he should ever do.

He cleared his throat and stared at the wall above the sink. "What are you making anyway?"

"Chicken fajitas. I have to use up all of the chicken in my freezer somehow. Hope you and Tate are hungry."

"Tate won't eat. He'll mow your grass and hit the guest room couch to sleep. He has to be up tonight while I catch a couple of hours." *Or try to.* Now that the house had been targeted again, sleep would probably be harder to come by than ever.

Jessica leaned heavily against the counter, seeming as exhausted as Sean felt. "Is anyone else I should know about prowling around my house? Is some mysterious person going to show up to paint my shutters next?"

Sean shook his head, lips pressed together to keep from laughing at that look on her face. At this point, anything was possible.

She got that sarcastic spark that said she'd fallen into the game with him. "Too bad. Those things need to be painted and I'm really having trouble getting excited about doing it myself."

"Maybe we can persuade Tate that shutter painting is the new lawn mowing?"

Jessica shrugged and went back to her food prep. "Maybe we should go out there and take the mower away from him and try it ourselves. Might yield some answers to some of these questions."

Questions like why Andrew Murphy's photo was on that cell phone…why Channing's killer had seen fit to destroy her body to the point that only DNA could identify her…and why Channing's belongings from her room simply didn't add up.

"You're thinking about Channing, aren't you?" Jessica had stopped what she was doing again, this time to watch him.

It was scary how she could read his mind. Sean studied a faint crack in the ceiling that ran from above the stove to a spot above the refrigerator, a mark likely left as the house settled over time. All it did was make him think this case was cracking him up.

"Are you also thinking what I'm thinking, that our Channing might not actually be Channing?" Jessica's voice hit home once again.

"Well, Kyle Randall sure isn't a soldier." Sean dragged a hand down his face and hazarded a look at her. "I don't know what I think anymore. They destroyed Channing's body, purposely did away with anything recognizable including fingerprints, and tried to destroy DNA. That's either exceptionally brutal, or someone is hiding something."

"You've got a slim bit of circumstantial evidence there. Surplus store uniforms and a charred body don't mean we're dealing with a fake."

"It does sort of sound like a movie plot." Something teased the edge of his mind, something that wouldn't fully form, something that felt like the one piece that could fit the whole puzzle together. But his mind was too tired to hang on to more than the edges of the thought.

He shoved it aside. "The bigger question is what their endgame is."

"And why they want me dead. They're bound to know that the phone is in your hands now, that everything I've seen and know has been passed on. Their own man is in custody. Killing me at this point gains them nothing." She backed away from the counter. "Maybe you can walk away from me now and figure this out without my help. Nobody's made an attempt on me today. Maybe they're done."

They were far from done, but he wasn't about to tell Jessica. She'd want to know why he thought that way, and he didn't want to give her reason to be afraid. She'd been nothing but a loose end to these guys at first, someone who could identify them. Now, it was personal, and that made the game much deadlier. "I'm not willing to take that chance."

He had a growing hunch, one that refused to stop nagging him. This might not be about her at all. He pulled his phone from his pocket and held it up. "I'll be back in a minute." Walking into the living room, he punched in Ashley's number.

She answered on the first ring. "You'd better be calling to tell me you're headed back here where it's safe."

"And hello to you, too, Ash."

She blew out an exasperated sigh. "Don't mess with me, Sean. Kyle Randall knows something. You can't—"

"Do me a favor." If he let her keep talking, she'd lecture him worse than his mama ever had. Sean had no intention of going into hiding, not while Jessica was in danger.

There was a stretch of silence as Ashley considered whether to grant him a favor or to keep yelling at him.

Finally, she sighed. "Fine. You're not going underground. What do you need?"

"That hacker's signature you found on Dylan's desktop?"

"No match for it in the major databases yet. What's up?"

"Run it against the hack on my computer in Afghanistan." He had to force the words out through a throat that didn't want to say them. He'd missed that hack and it had almost cost both of them their lives.

"Sean. No."

"Do it, Ash. Leave no stone unturned."

"But if it's the same hacker, that means we didn't win. People who worked with Mina are still out there and your guy Randall..."

"Is working for them."

She didn't say another word, but the clicks coming through the line as she tapped on her keyboard spoke a Morse code of anxiety. Sean had once encoded data using a program he'd devised with Ashley, and he'd made her the key. When Sam Mina's minions hacked his computer and found out he wasn't who he pretended to be, they snatched him and went after Ashley. Only Ethan's quick thinking had been able to save both of them.

If those coded signatures matched, it meant this wasn't over—they weren't safe. And it explained why the bad guys had targeted Jessica.

The clicking stopped along with all other sounds on the line.

"Ash?"

"Sean. I—" She cleared her throat. "The signatures match. Mina's men are still active."

Heat, a mixture of fear and anger, flooded Sean from the inside out. Sean's mind and body had paid the price in a takedown of Sam Mina's terror cell last year. Those men had tried to destroy him, but he'd survived and defeated them. Clearly, someone wanted revenge. "They're coming after Jessica to get to me."

THIRTEEN

Sean stretched his arms wide along the rail of the covered back porch, leaning out to stare up at the dark Tennessee sky. He'd come out here when sleep eluded him and he had to convince himself the backyard wasn't full of men climbing to the roof.

Worse, the house had grown too claustrophobic, driving him outside in a search for something he couldn't define. With Jessica's roommate gone to visit her parents for the holiday, Sean felt comfortable roaming out of the den for the first time. He'd sent Tate out front to stand his watch there, wanting to stand guard and needing the quiet and the darkness to unknot everything.

Out here near the river, his back to Clarksville, the stars hung low and bright. The temperature had risen over the past few days, leaving the night warm enough for a sweatshirt and jeans, but his breath still frosted. It would be awesome to be a kid again, sitting in the tree stand near his dad, pretending to be a dragon who could level a forest with one blow.

What he wouldn't give to burn away the chaff and get to the center of whatever was happening now. He'd incinerate the fear that ate at his shoulder and made the scars on his arms raw. If Mina's men laid their hands on him again, he'd never get out alive, even if his heart was still beating.

The back door popped open, and Sean held the rail tighter but didn't turn. He'd half expected her.

"Hey." Jessica's voice came from behind him as the wood floorboards creaked her presence. "You okay out here?"

"I'm fine. And you should be upstairs asleep. It's after midnight." The way he was feeling tonight, he didn't need her close by. He was too tired, too worried, to keep his guard up around her. It was way too likely he'd fire off at the mouth and tell her all of the things he was beginning to feel.

"I could say the same to you." She stepped to the rail just out of reach and held out a steaming mug. "If you're going to freeze out here, you might as well be warm."

She was wearing black Army sweats and the gray University of Tennessee sweatshirt she seemed to think was a security blanket. The clothes softened her. Did she realize, with her hair pulled back in that loose ponytail, she looked more like a college freshman than a seasoned soldier?

He took the cup, careful not to brush her fingers. It would be too much. "So why aren't you asleep?"

"Same reason you aren't." She took a sip from her own mug and stared out at the yard. "Trying to figure out everything. I wish I had a huge poster board and some markers." She drew an imaginary square in the air. "I could put everything on a flat surface and see if any dots connect." She tilted her head back and stared up at the sky. "I love it out here."

"Yeah?" Sean held his coffee between his hands and watched her, her neck stretched out, her face relaxing as she leaned over the rail to look up at the sky. Every time she appeared, the nightmares receded and the world came into focus. Even now, with his failures staring him in the face, Jessica made him feel he could somehow be whole again.

"Yeah. On a clear night like this, there's nothing like it." She set her coffee on the rail. "Makes me want to find my sleeping bag and lay out in the backyard all night, watching the stars."

Sounded like a great idea to him. And one he shouldn't follow up on, not if he wanted to keep his distance and keep her safe. "It's nothing like the stars in Afghanistan, though. When things got bad, I used to step outside and look up. It was so dark out there the stars seemed so close you could touch them."

She chuckled softly. "You sound like me. It was hard to believe the same stars there were in the sky over this very house. It made home not so far away, but it made the war that much worse, thinking people could be sleeping in freedom half a world away while we fought in the mud and the snow and the blood." She shot him a sheepish grin. "I sound like a teenage girl."

She looked like one, too. He hid a smile in his coffee mug. "Nah. You sound like a homesick soldier."

"Is that why you're out here now? Homesick? Or something else?" She turned and leaned a hip against the rail, facing him in a way that said she was about to ask questions she would no longer let him evade. "You didn't eat after you made that phone call earlier, and you prowled like a caged animal the rest of the evening. Now you're out here contemplating astronomy instead of sleeping. Talk to me, Turner. Whatever's going on, it affects my life, too, and I can handle it."

He didn't doubt that. She'd proven she could deal with

anything these guys threw at her. But this wasn't about her. It was about him, and if he started talking…

"I need to know."

The words were low and pleading, the tone washing over Sean's skin with a warmth he couldn't fight. He surrendered. "Last year, I was assigned to gather intelligence on a group that was hacking into our computers to skim money. What I found pointed to a contractor who was funneling money into a terror cell. The problem was, they were better than I thought they were, and they hacked into my system and figured out I'd found them." He'd been cocky, arrogant enough to think his skills outpaced theirs. If he'd been a little more humble, he'd have seen the signs before it was too late. "We thought we'd shut down their operation, but we were wrong. The same people who hacked my computer in Afghanistan hacked yours. And it looks like, since they know I'm involved, they're rewriting their own script. They want retaliation."

Jessica's attention dropped to her coffee mug. She sat it on the rail and swallowed hard. "What do you mean?"

"I knew there was a likelihood I'd get found out overseas, so I mailed data back to Ashley. When they hacked me, they found out and went after her. I failed to protect Ashley, and it's something I've never been able to live down. Now they know I'm supposed to be protecting you."

"So even though Kyle Randall has been arrested and I'm no longer the only one who can identify them, they came after me to send a message to you."

The edge to her voice sliced his heart. "What they want to do is worse than killing me, and if I drop the investigation, they might leave you alone." Or kill her anyway, if they ever realized how much she was starting to mean to him.

"You can't do that."

"I know. We don't negotiate with terrorists." He tried to ignore the tightness in his chest. "But they want to reinforce the fact they're not happy I messed with them and that we haven't won yet. They're trying to prove a point." *That I'm a danger to everyone I care about.*

"This is personal for you." She edged closer until she was almost touching him. Even from that distance, her warmth transferred between them, palpable on his arm. "What did they do to you?"

He tensed at her nearness and shifted to the side, putting distance between them but not stepping away. Other than his debriefing, he hadn't told anyone what had happened, and he hadn't even told the full truth then. Everyone would judge him, would treat him with wariness or pity, as if he was some kind of wounded animal.

But it was festering inside him, and answering Jessica Dylan's question seemed like the only medicine that would stop the pain. He wanted to maintain silence, but something enveloped them and shut out the rest of the world, creating a place where he was safe to air everything. "By the time I figured out they were on to me and I warned Ashley, it was too late. They dressed as Afghan soldiers and took me off the COP. They figured out I'd used Ashley as the cipher for the data I'd encrypted, so they tried to take her, too. She was the only one who could decode the files. They brought me back to the States to use us as leverage against each other." He turned to the low porch ceiling, chest tight. "If it hadn't been for Ethan, she'd be dead." Ethan had been able to get to Ashley in time to pull her from an assassin's grasp, but that hadn't stopped the bad guys from coming at her again and again. When Ethan's partner was revealed as a double agent, it had nearly been the end of all their lives.

"Ashley's not dead." Jessica inched closer, but she didn't touch him. "She's safe, moving on. And you're not. What did they do that keeps you from sleeping and from…trusting?"

A day's worth of beard scratched against Sean's fingers as he dragged his hand across his mouth and gripped his chin. He couldn't tell her. It wasn't fair to let his nightmares become hers. The visions swirled in his stomach, heightening the acidity in the coffee and twisting like a knife. Even now, here, in the clear air of her back porch, he could smell burning flesh, feel heat that defied description, that burned so intensely white-hot on his skin it made him sweat cold. Their threats toward Jessica only intensified the memories.

"It's okay." Her voice came in a whisper so low, he could barely hear it.

He dropped his hands to the rail in front of him and held on tight, the jagged edges of the wood digging splinters into his fingers. He couldn't tell her.

But if he didn't, the images might kill him.

His eyes drifted shut. "They shot me. In the shoulder. Point blank." His captors had been trying to send a message to Ethan and Ashley, a message that said they'd stop at nothing. Sean had tried to bite back the scream, tried to keep Ethan from hearing over the phone, but he couldn't. It was too much on a mind already stretched to its thinnest, on a body already broken. "But I never told them anything to compromise the mission."

"You wouldn't. It's not in you to give up." She said it as if she believed it, believed him. "What else?"

She didn't ask out of curiosity, nor out of pity, but out of something that said she wanted to understand, wanted to know why he ticked the way he did. And just as he'd never wanted anyone else to know before, Sean needed Jessica to know.

Everything. He needed her to know everything about him—good, bad, mediocre. All of it.

Letting go of the rail, afraid he'd fly off the earth without an anchor, he shoved the sleeves of his sweatshirt to his elbows and held out his arms. There was no going back.

The scars shone faintly in the moonlight, crisscrossing in lines smoother than the rest of his skin.

Jessica gasped softly. "They burned you."

Among other things. "With a metal rod."

Her fingers inched closer, hesitated, then she cupped his hand in hers and traced the longest scar that ran diagonally from his elbow to his wrist. Her fingers sent chills up his arms, but not the kind from his nightmares.

These were another thing entirely. He watched her fingers, then followed her arm up to her eyes.

She was looking at him, not at his scars, in a way that said she knew him better than either of them thought she did, that said she could read everything he wasn't saying. "You're stronger than you think you are."

"No." He hated weakness, had never wanted one soul's pity. He didn't deserve it for what he'd done to Ashley. He deserved the pain he'd endured, every beating, every burn. The whole thing was his fault.

But he couldn't make himself pull away from the comfort he found with Jessica Dylan.

Her grip tightened on his hand as she laid her fingers flat on his arm, covering his scars. She leaned closer. "You are." He read the words on her lips more than he heard them.

She believed that. Made him want to believe it, too. He wanted that kind of faith, wanted it deep inside, where she was starting to make him believe she could chase the nightmares away.

For the first time since the back wall of his office blew out, he was in the moment, in the reality of life, and it wasn't crushing him. He didn't have to be fully on guard.

Jessica Dylan made him feel as if he hadn't died that day.

He ought to back away, but he couldn't. If he did, he'd be cold. Death would creep back in. He needed her, and if he took this step forward, he could never, ever take it back.

He slipped his hand from hers and reached up to lay his fingers against her cheeks, feeling tears there. And without caring about the consequences, needing to prolong that sensation of warmth and life, he pressed a kiss to her forehead, then found her mouth and kissed her, trying to take in the spark inside of her to relight his own.

Jessica wrapped her arms around Sean's neck and pulled him closer, deepening the moment, drawing it out, trying to erase the memories of what he'd told her. He needed to feel here and now, safe. She could protect him, comfort him, love him if he'd let her.

And she wanted to, more than anything.

When he broke the kiss, she held on tighter and pressed her cheek to his, trying to communicate without words that his past was over, that right now he was safe. That, to the best of her ability, she would never let anything hurt him again.

That she had somehow managed to fall soul deep in love with him.

For a long moment he let her hold him, seeming to relax and sink into the peace she was offering. Then he straightened, set his hands on her shoulders and stepped back, opening a distance between them that filled with the cool night air and seeped through her sweatshirt, under her skin and into her heart.

"This can't happen." Sean took another step away and ran his hand along the back of his neck, shaking his head. "We can't do this."

"You can't let them win by living in what they did to you." His regret tore through her heart. All the times she'd sensed he was in pain, she'd never dreamed it was a brokenness this deep. "You can't keep hurting alone."

"And I can't involve you, either." He dropped his hand and gestured toward the darkness filling her backyard. "These people will kill you. Right now, they're only after you because they know I'm the one protecting you. They think they can undermine me by proving to me I can't function as a soldier, that I can't complete the mission, that I can't protect the ones I...I care about. They play psychological games and they want me to suffer." He dropped his hand to his side and shook his head again, as if he was trying to throw off a vision. "Jess, if they suspect for one moment that you're important to me in any way, they won't just kill you. They'll torture you in ways that your nightmares never even imagined. The things they threatened to do to Ashley were horrible and unspeakable, and she was only a friend, not... If they figure out that I..." He walked to the other side of the porch and stared down the street toward the river.

That you what? She'd never wanted anyone to finish a sentence more in her whole life. *Say it. Say you love me.*

There was no way to deny her heart had gone out to him almost from the moment she first saw him. Tonight, his confession—it all amped everything to emotions that should be impossible for the short time they'd known each other.

But she couldn't deny them. She loved him. And there he stood, on the edge of telling her he felt the same, yet he was letting terrorists rob them of their lives. "You can't live like this."

He turned his head up toward the sky. "Tell me about it."

"You can't live in fear of them forever."

He laughed, the sound brittle in the rapidly cooling air. "Funny thing is, it's not them I'm afraid of. It's me." His posture stiffened under his dark blue sweatshirt. "I sleep, and I see them. The minute my guard drops and I start to relax, they're there." He finally turned back to her, and the desperate look on his face nearly stopped her heart. "Do you know what it's like to be terrified that if you go to sleep, you'll wake up right back in a living nightmare? Your mind never drops its guard." He sniffed. "I can't remember the last time I got solid rest. I'm scared, Jess. Scared I'm going to lose my mind. Scared that if the Army finds out, they'll chapter me out as unfit. Scared that…"

"That what?" She stayed in place, even though she wanted to go to him and make this all better somehow.

"That if I let go and I let myself…feel this thing…that if I feel something for you and you're ever in danger and I have to save you, I won't be able to. That the stakes will be too high, and I'll freeze up and lose you forever."

There was nothing to say. No words. What he was saying didn't compute into anything with an answer. Sean had bought the lie that he was weak, broken, unworthy.

"I can't feel anything. I won't. There's too much to lose if I do. The only way to keep you safe from them and from me is to keep you at a distance." He broke contact and headed for the back door. "I need to get you back inside. For all I know, they're watching us right now. And if they are…"

If they were, that kiss had given the enemy every-thing they needed to destroy both of them. But none of that mattered.

It was one thing to die on the outside, to have your physical being eradicated, but a whole other thing to let your soul be slaughtered, and Sean was standing on the edge of that death even now. Desperation sparked against Jessica's skin. "Seems to me you're relying a whole lot on Sean Turner and not nearly enough on God." It was true. Sean couldn't do it on his own, and she couldn't do it for him, either. The clarity of that thought hit harder than his kiss had earlier.

"God?" He stopped halfway to the door, his back to her, and laughed. "Don't even."

The tone of his voice was colder than the air around her, chilling her from the inside out. "What are you say-ing?"

He turned to face her, as dead in his eyes as if she'd shot him. "That God couldn't care less, Dylan."

The words were a physical blow to the gut. Jessica took a step back. It had never occurred to her that Sean didn't share her faith. To hear him put it so boldly tight-ened her insides in physical pain, the rejection of her Sav-ior personal. "What? Are you saying He doesn't exist?"

His lip curled. "I'm saying He doesn't care. It's pretty clear He exists." He waved a hand toward the sky. "None of that happened by accident. But does He care?" Sean shook his head and shoved his hands into the pocket of his sweatshirt. "Not one bit. If He did, my life would have turned out a whole lot different. Both of our lives would have turned out a whole lot different."

"Sean…"

"Explain it to me then. If He cares so much, why kill my parents? Not just my parents, but the couple I thought of as a second family? Why let Ashley get shot and then, just when she was healing, let her get an infection that nearly killed her? Then leave her riddled with fear that robbed her of her career and sent her down a life marked by Plan B? Why let me get not just taken but…" He waved away the words. "Never mind. You get the point."

"I really don't." Jessica felt the sting of tears, but where they came from was too muddled to understand. "It sounds to me like you had two parents who loved you and a bonus family besides. Some of us are lucky to get one. One parent who thinks we're worth something."

"Jess…" His posture relaxed as though he realized he'd crossed a line.

"No. He gave you Ashley as your family. He saved her, and out of that mess He gave her Ethan. He saved you. And out of this mess, there's a better thing coming. You're not dead yet. In case you missed it, you're still breathing."

He pulled himself straighter, the wall between them growing with the motion. "Am I?"

"You were two minutes ago." There was no doubt. Her lips were still too warm. "If you're not now, it's because you're holding your breath and wishing to die."

His face tensed and he jerked open the door. "Get inside, Jess. This conversation's over."

FOURTEEN

Sean sat straight up on the couch, kicking at the blankets tangled around his legs, cold sweat coating his skin. What was that noise? His breath came hard, and he fought for rhythm, finally getting his lungs to work in his favor.

The house was silent, lit softly by the just-risen sun edging through the curtains. He pulled his sweatshirt straight and dragged his hand across his eyes. How long had he been asleep? He glanced at his watch. Three hours? Three blessedly uninterrupted hours?

He sat back against the couch, swiping the sweat from his brow. Three hours and no nightmares. Spilling his guts had been good—even if it was the worst mistake he'd ever made. The wounded hurt in Jessica's expression when he'd told her God had checked out of his life had almost made him take back everything he'd said so he could pull her close again.

What if Jessica was right? He'd lain awake turning her words over for what felt like hours before succumbing to the heaviest sleep in recent memory. If only he could go back to that blessedly dark place and not have to face her this morning.

A click drifted from the front door. Sean sat up and

eased toward his gun on the coffee table, not wanting to move too fast and alert the person on the other side of the door to his presence.

"It's me." Tate's voice crept around the opening, chased by his hand and then the rest of his body as he slipped in and shut the door. "Hold your fire." He grinned around the words.

Sean relaxed and propped his feet up on the coffee table, hoping to act as if nothing had happened the night before, as if everything was exactly the same as it had been when he'd booted Tate out of the backyard last night, even though the world had shifted and would never return to its normal axis. He'd said too much, watched any chance he had with Jessica burn into ashes when he told her everything—when he told her God didn't care. That confusion, that hurt... She'd never respect him again.

And it was for the best.

Tate was not the kind of guy to buy into an act. "You slept?" He stopped and arched an eyebrow, waiting for Sean to confess something.

Too late. Sean had already confessed everything, and it had only made things worse. Still, he wasn't going to give Tate any more than the man had asked for. "Yeah. I got some rack time, believe it or not."

"Took me forever to figure out what the noise from the living room was." Tate stretched and touched the ceiling, stifling a yawn. "I circled the house twice before I figured out you were in here inhaling the wallpaper."

Sean scratched his neck. "I do not snore." That could be deadly in the field.

"No, you don't. But you also don't sleep so sound you missed me coming into the house around four-thirty.

For half a second, I almost checked your pulse because I thought you were dead."

Ironic, since last night was the first time Sean had felt alive in nearly a year. And he'd had to put himself right back into his own tomb.

"That's a nasty look on your face. Worse than your usual." Tate stopped at the head of the hallway on his way to the office, where he was bunking on a daybed. "You okay? Or is it that you don't know how to act with a couple of hours of sleep tucked in your pocket?"

"That's it. My brain hasn't adjusted yet." Sean had opened his mouth enough the past two days. Tate didn't need to be on the receiving end of his confessions, too.

"Run out of grass to kill, Tate?" Jessica's voice drifted up the hallway, and Tate turned to meet it while Sean's heart picked up a notch. He dug his hands into the hardwood and willed his pulse to stop acting without orders.

"Yeah. I'm going to outsource to the neighbors next. This mess of spaghetti you guys are digging through is going to take a whole city block's worth of lawns to sort out." He threw up a hand to the as-yet-invisible Jessica and called back to Sean, "I'm passing the torch to you for the day. Last night was long and boring. See you guys this evening."

Sean didn't answer. Long? Yes. Disastrously life changing? Yes. Boring? No.

There was a mumbled conversation as Jessica and Tate passed each other in the hallway.

Sean shoved the blankets to the foot of the couch and stood, grateful he'd racked out in his sweatshirt and jeans. At least he looked halfway alert. It was nearly six-thirty. He'd have to get dressed quick if he was going to go in to work with Jessica. She'd likely be annoyed on top of her pain if he made her late.

Jessica hesitated at the end of the hallway, stopping at the sight of him. She caught his eyes, then flicked her gaze away toward the kitchen. She shoved her bangs out of her face and tugged at the hem of her plaid flannel shirt. "Morning." The greeting was dull and directed at the dining room table.

"Morning." Something wasn't quite right. The Jessica he'd become acquainted with hated being late for work, hated anything that made her superiors think less of her. Yet, right now, with the clock dangerously close to departure time, she was wearing jeans and a purple flannel button-down, poking around as though she had hours. Had last night's conversation been too much for her? Had he broken Jessica Dylan? "Why aren't you in uniform?"

"It's Thursday." She didn't stop walking; just let her voice trail her as she disappeared into the kitchen. Running water and clattering glass drifted on the tail of her statement.

It's Thursday? Great. All he needed was more riddles. Sean scratched his cheek, the stubble scraping his fingertips. He edged around the corner to peek through the kitchen door, half-afraid she was going to haul a frying pan at his head.

But no. She was measuring grounds into the coffee-maker.

His mind might still be foggy from the unaccustomed sleep, but this was definitely out of the ordinary. "Jess... Jessica." He had no idea how to address her after last night. He'd probably lost the right to *Jess* forever. Maybe even to Jessica. But doing a complete reverse to calling her Staff Sergeant Dylan? No. It sounded ridiculous. "What does Thursday have to do with anything?"

She stopped spooning coffee and stared at him in a

way that made him wonder if he'd grown a second head. "It's a DONSA."

A day of no scheduled activities. Those usually fell on Fridays or Mondays. "On a Thursday." He was drawing this out, but at least asking inane questions kept her talking to him. And even three-word answers felt better than picking up where they'd left off last night.

"It's Thanksgiving. You know—turkey and stuffing and pumpkin pie?"

Oh, yeah. Sean dropped his shoulder against the door frame. With everything else taking up space in his head, he'd forgotten.

"I'm behind on cooking, not that it matters. There's no one coming over anyway." She scooped in two more spoonfuls of coffee and dropped the lid. "Tate said you slept last night."

Really? One good night's shut-eye and the whole world acted as if the news should interrupt programming.

"Wipe that look off your face. It's a big deal when Sean Turner gets a good…" She faltered, pressing the button on the coffeemaker and watching it come to life. "I'm glad you rested." Her smile didn't quite reach her eyes as she pushed the machine away from the edge of the cabinet and pulled open the refrigerator door, staring inside.

Sean ran his tongue along the inside of his cheek. The elephant standing between them took up every inch of space in the kitchen. They couldn't act as though nothing had happened, as if he hadn't let himself fall into the dream he'd had almost since the first moment he saw her, as if he hadn't pulled away and cut her to the center of who she was by denying everything she believed. "Listen. About what happened. I—"

The bottles on the fridge door rattled as Jessica

slammed it shut, then stood with her fingers gripping the handle, staring at the stainless steel. "There's no reason to talk about what happened. You made yourself perfectly clear."

Sean tilted his head toward the ceiling and exhaled loudly. "Jess…"

"I get it." The tone of her voice changed, though it didn't exactly soften. "But that doesn't mean I like it."

He tipped his head until he found her watching him.

She drew her tongue along her bottom lip. "I understand everything except you blaming God. It goes against everything I know to be true. And I can't… I just can't grasp that. I can't hear that without hurting for you. But then again…" She pulled the refrigerator open for a second time and reached for the milk, her mouth drawn into a confused frown. "Then again I've never been in your shoes, so I guess there's no way for me to ever really understand." She reached up and pulled two coffee mugs from hooks beneath the cabinet. "I just want the chance to try."

He ached to give her that chance. Even after last night's blowout, even though the consequences were literally life and death, he wanted to close the space between them and give her the chance. Even if peace only existed for five minutes in the space of this kitchen, he wanted to pull her to him again. His legs ached with the effort of keeping his feet in place. He opened his mouth to say something, anything, but her phone shattered the long stretch of emptiness between them.

She shook her head and pulled it from her pocket, checking the screen before answering. "Good morning, Major Braden." She listened for a moment, then thunked one of the coffee mugs hard on the counter. "I'll be right there."

"What?" Sean's feet moved forward of their own volition.

"That was the rear detachment commander. They found a body in the river closer to downtown. A female." She finally looked up, weariness coating her words. "Wearing Channing's uniform."

"No, the families of our deployed soldiers don't need to know any details. Captain Alexander wants no comments on Private Murphy's death other than the bare facts. He stepped on an IED." Jessica pinched the bridge of her nose and stared at the scarred wooden top of her desk, tracing a scratch with her thumb. They'd arrived at the building before the commander, and Jessica had made the mistake of answering her phone. "There's nothing more going on."

"What do you want me to say about the rumors swirling about Murphy? Because there's been no official word, I've heard some crazy theories." Trina Stewart, the Family Readiness Support Assistant who acted as the liaison between the wives and the chain of command blew out a sigh. "It's Thanksgiving, Staff Sergeant. I want to be screaming at football on TV and stuffing myself until I'm miserable, not fielding phone calls about conspiracy theories. I've gotten a dozen calls today if I've gotten one."

"I'm sure. My office voice mail is full." Jessica sat back and stretched tight neck muscles. Between multiple threats on her life and one big threat to her heart, her nerves were stretched tighter than guitar strings.

Trina didn't wait for her to say more. "I'm also getting questions about whether or not Specialist Channing was murdered."

"What? Why would anyone ask that? She was only here temporarily before heading overseas. Nobody here even knows her, and how in the world would the families have heard something happened to her? We just got word yesterday." Just wait until the families got wind of a body in the river wearing Specialist Channing's uniform. Then things would really get out of control.

Trina chuckled. "If you put your ear to the ground around here, it hums with gossip and guessing."

True. Especially when it came to deployed or soon-to-be-deployed soldiers. "Listen—" Jessica stopped as Sean tapped on her door frame and waited for permission to enter. She hadn't seen him since they got to post, and his sudden appearance did something to her knees that made her glad she was sitting behind her desk. "Hey, Trina. I'll have to call you back." She clicked End without saying goodbye.

Jessica arched an eyebrow and waited, shoving down the memory of the kiss that had washed over all he'd said after.

Following the commander's call, Sean hadn't picked up the conversation about their relationship again. In fact, other than a few cursory comments, they hadn't spoken since he walked out of the kitchen to get ready. It was as though their entire relationship had been set backward to before they met. No. Worse than that. Things had been a whole lot easier a few days ago than they were now. They'd shared too much to reset to the beginning.

But you'd never know it now. First he was silent, then he'd vanished, and now that he'd returned, the look on his face... It wasn't one she'd ever seen before, and definitely not one she had the ability to read.

She worked to keep her own expression equally impassive. "Come in." She could play detached and unaffected too, even though the memory of his embrace still pulled her close, warming her from the inside out. Even though her fingers were still tender with the rough scars on his arms. If he wanted to keep her at arm's length, she'd let him. With his attitude toward God, distance was probably better that way anyway.

Since she'd met him, Sean had never been as hesitant as he was right now, slipping into the chair across from her desk as if he was half-afraid he wasn't actually welcome in the room.

Jessica didn't want to make it any easier on him, either. While the last thing she wanted was to let him know he'd wounded her with his disappearance, the kicked dog inside of her still wanted to bite. "Can I help you, Staff Sergeant?"

"So we're going by rank now?" His posture shifted and tightened with annoyance. He straightened in the chair. "Isn't that a little passive-aggressive?"

"Seemed like the right way to put that distance between us you seem to want." Okay. Too far. Those words smacked of the hurt that pulsed just under her skin.

He relaxed. "Listen, Jess, like I said earlier, I did a terrible job of explaining myself last night. I don't know that—"

"I thought you did a fine job. You're exactly right. You have a job to do, and so do I. It just so happens that the two jobs intersect. When our jobs are finished, we're finished. You can go back to Maryland and I can go on with…" She waved a hand in the air. With what? Even she had no idea what she wanted next. What her father wanted was abundantly clear, but what did she want for herself? After facing down terror in her own home, the desire to be her own person was growing. For the first time, what she wanted mattered.

Sean eyed her, waiting for her to finish. "It's not that."

"Then you've got about two minutes to explain, because the major will be here any—"

"The major is here now." The voice from the doorway held more authority than Sean's. Major Braden stood there, stone-faced and unreadable, clutching his phone in a white-knuckled grip. He cut an imposing figure, even dressed down in jeans and an orange sweater.

Jessica stood, and Sean glanced over his shoulder, then followed suit. "Sir."

The major stepped into the room. "I'm glad to see you brought Staff Sergeant Turner with you. The two of you should hear this together." He gestured for Sean and Jessica to sit as he dropped into the second chair in front of Jessica's desk, thumb tapping the cell phone in his hand.

So the major did have some indication of Sean's official presence here. She'd wondered how much Captain Alexander had passed up the chain. Jessica sat as the men made quick greetings.

The major held up his phone. His stark white hair and ice-blue eyes always made him intense and intimidating. Right now, it almost seemed he could freeze the device in his hand with nothing more than sheer willpower. "It seems we have more than one problem."

"Sir?" Jessica sat forward and gripped her knees tightly, trying to channel all of her energy into her fingers so her body and her face wouldn't reveal the strain. "Something besides Specialist Channing being dead in Colorado and someone else being found in the river wearing her uniform?"

A muscle tensed in Sean's jaw, but he didn't speak.

"The body in the river..." Major Braden rubbed the side of his nose. "I was sent a photo, one I'll spare showing you so as to avoid ruining your Thanksgiving dinner later. But that body was the woman who was here calling herself Lindsay Channing."

The coffee Jessica had gulped on the way over roiled in her stomach.

Sean sat back in his chair and ran his hands down the arms. "You're sure, sir?"

"As sure as I can be without actually going to the morgue for a face-to-face." He rolled his shoulders back and stiffened his chin. "I'm going to avoid that if I can."

Sean nodded. "What about fingerprint identification?"

"That's the thing." The tone of the major's voice changed, grew even more grave. "Her hands are missing."

The chair rolled backward, crashing against the wall as Jessica stiffened and stood, sure she was going to lose everything she'd eaten for the past week. She swallowed hard twice and pulled in deep breaths. This was starting to sound like a horror movie. "What?"

Sean's thumb beat double time on the wooden arm of the chair. "Someone didn't care if the authorities recognized her face. But they sure did care if her identity could be easily tracked."

The room swirled around Jessica. The woman they'd thought was Lindsay Channing was murdered just like the soldier she was impersonating. "So have we ever met the woman in Colorado?"

"I don't know." The major shook his head. "I called the detective out there this morning after seeing the photo of the woman in the river, and he had more to add to our mystery. They found the body of the real Specialist Channing several weeks ago. There was a delay getting DNA testing done."

"So our Channing killed the real Channing and took her place here," Sean said. "We have to figure out why."

"But like I said, we have more than one problem."

Jessica's shoulders sank, the weight of everything too heavy. She wanted to get in her car and drive until she ran out of gas, then walk until she collapsed. Nowhere was too far away right now. Nowhere.

"Sir, I need to know what you know." Sean sat forward, taking control of the situation from the ranking officer.

The major nodded and aimed a finger at Jessica's desk phone. "I've got the casualty assistance officer, the one we sent to Specialist Murphy's family, on hold on my office line. Lieutenant Parker found out something you need to hear. If you'll bring him up on speaker, Staff Sergeant Dylan."

Jessica's gut iced over. She couldn't handle much more. If Major Braden wanted Sean in here, this meant their puzzle was about to gain some more random, unfittable pieces. She pressed the two necessary buttons and cleared her throat. "Lieutenant Parker? This is Staff Sergeant Dylan. I have Major Braden and Staff Sergeant Sean Turner in the room with me."

"Staff Sergeant Dylan." The lieutenant's voice carried a strain that tugged at Jessica's stomach muscles even more. "Staff Sergeant Turner."

The major leaned forward, focused on the phone. "Lieutenant, fill the staff sergeants in on what you told me."

"Sir, I went to Specialist Murphy's aunt's house and we chatted a bit about her nephew. She pulled out his graduation picture as she talked and, well... The picture she showed me is not Specialist Murphy. At least, he looks nothing like the photo you sent."

Jessica jerked her head back. She couldn't help it. Fear heated her skin.

Sean looked driven, angry, and far from surprised. "This is Staff Sergeant Sean Turner. Did you show his aunt the pictures we sent with you?"

"Yes, sir. Mrs. Murphy said she'd never seen either of those soldiers in her whole life."

FIFTEEN

"I can't think anymore." Jessica paced in the small courtyard surrounded by the battalion's low brick buildings, clenching and unclenching her fists. "It's too much."

Sean stood in front of a memorial statue, watching her make the back-and-forth trek between a stone bench and the monument next to the one where he stood. His feet itched to pace right along with her, but if he showed restlessness, the two of them would only feed off each other until the only thing they accomplished was blisters on their toes. When the major had returned to his office to try to find more information on their dead suspects, Jessica had fled the room, claiming she was desperate for fresh air.

Sean couldn't blame her. He'd hoped the chill of the November morning and the slight warmth of the Tennessee sunshine would jog something in either one of their minds. So far, nothing. Nothing but her pacing and him restless to join her.

Stopping on the farthest point of her route from him, Jessica turned and threw her hands out. "I've got nothing." She dropped her hands to her sides. "What is going on here?"

"Start talking. Maybe we'll sort the whole thing out."

The words seemed to wrap around Jessica and bind her hands to her sides. She stared at him for a long moment, trying to read something behind the words.

Sort the whole thing out. In the middle of confusion and more questions than answers, had they both defaulted back to their relationship, to what happened on her porch last night? He'd give anything to take that moment back, but he couldn't. And sooner or later they'd have to deal with it. But now was definitely not the time.

Jessica seemed to hear his thoughts. She took one step forward. "Okay, two dead soldiers who aren't actually soldiers, and one dead soldier who was being impersonated by one of our wannabes." She threw out her arms again. "See? Nothing."

"So we have fake identities. At least two." Sean straightened and pressed two fingers into his temple. There was that nagging thought again, the one he couldn't quite grasp and pull out of the swirl.

Sinking to the small bench, Jessica turned her eyes to the sky. "Do you know what it would take to create an entire fake identity for a soldier? What databases you'd have to hack into and how you'd have to build an entire life? You're talking driver's licenses, birth certificates, high school transcripts, test scores...not to mention awards, evaluations, schools like basic or airborne. You can hack a lot of things, but it would be next to impossible to create every document necessary to support an entire fake career."

She had a point. Creating a fake Enlisted Records Brief would be easy, but carefully building every piece to back it up would be time-consuming even for one soldier. For multiple? Hardly worth the trouble. "I'm not sure we're talking a complete fabrication. After all, somewhere out there is a real, live, walking and talking Andrew Murphy. His next of kin confirmed his existence, even has graduation photos and prom pictures."

"You hope he's still alive," Jessica muttered.

He did. He fervently did. "What if our perps didn't fake an entire identity, but simply stole one?"

"Even that would be a stretch. You'd have to have the ability to hack into the system and replace all kinds of identifying information, including..." Jessica gasped.

"Photos." Sean finished the sentence for her. "You'd have to have a way to replace the photos."

Jessica stood. "The pictures on our fake Channing's phone were all Department of Defense ID card photos. She was the ringleader."

"No." Sean scanned the area around them. "If that's true, who killed her? I'm going to guess they cut her hands off to avoid easy identification from fingerprints and were hoping she'd decompose or be lost in the river so DNA couldn't be run. Her real identity must link her back to their leader somehow. As for the real Channing, they clearly wanted to keep her unidentified so that no one would find her and expose the fake."

"They chose the perfect timing to do it, too. She was young, not in the Army long, coming to a new unit... Nobody would know what she looked like. And if she managed to get a new ID card, no one would question her." Jessica shook her head. "Very smart."

Sean studied the windows of the headquarters building. "So they keep the records and switch out photos, get new IDs...that's a serious hack. And it runs some serious risk."

"How so?"

"Chances of getting caught are high. If you die, the whole thing unravels quickly. Not to mention, if you get injured..." Sean's mouth tried to drop right open on him.

Everything was starting to make sense. "How did you tell me Murphy died?"

"He stepped on an IED."

"No. You said he had a reaction to a blood transfusion and his body was too weak to handle it. What kind of reaction?"

Jessica raised her hand and shook her head, seeming even more confused. "No idea. Why?"

"Your fake Murphy was treated based on the real Murphy's medical records. His dog tags and his uniform would have had the real Murphy's blood type on them. If his blood type was different…"

"He'd have had an ABO incompatibility reaction. Blood clots. Stroke. Kidney failure."

"They'd have written it off as mislabeled donor blood." Their Murphy had died needlessly, playing Russian roulette with his life. "They gambled on nothing happening to themselves, and, if it did, no one caring enough to view the body. Neither Channing nor Murphy had any family to speak of, not close enough to raise questions if the real soldiers went missing."

"And based on the real Channing's records, she only had that one distant friend." Jessica snapped her fingers. "We need to contact her. See if that friend recognizes the photo of our fake or if she has any pictures of the real Channing." She stepped quickly for her office.

Sean grabbed her bicep. "Slow your roll. Let's think this through. You don't know if the friend is in on this. It's highly unlikely but, for all you know, she's the one who killed the real Channing. We can't tip our hand."

Jessica huffed a sigh. "Okay, so now what?"

"We've still got the guy who drove Channing's getaway car out there. I'm going to guess he's somewhere close, and unless he's dead himself, he may be the one who put that body in the river. If he's in deep enough, he may already have his credentials lined up and be able to move freely on and off the base. I have to get you home. You're not safe."

"But what about—"

"You. Safe. First. Then we'll worry about what's next." Sean glanced at his watch. Almost noon. "We'll get Tate in on this and figure out their endgame."

Jessica took a step back, dropping Sean's hands from her arms. "Do you realize what this means?"

Sean nodded, gut twisting in dread. Everything had just gone way above his head. There were dozens...dozens of photos on that phone. And if each one represented an imposter who'd managed to slip into the ranks undetected, who knew what they could be planning. Bombings on outposts, murders of individual soldiers... The end result could be high body counts and a military that fell apart at the seams when brother stopped trusting brother.

The endgame could be the end of their military.

"What do we do?" Jessica fell into step beside Sean as they walked back toward the headquarters building. This was so big. Too big. At least two fake soldiers had infiltrated her company. If there were dozens of soldiers dispersed across dozens of bases and units... "Without names, we can't go looking them up. We'd have to have a way to run facial recognition on every single ID in the system. That's impossible."

Sean pulled the door open and motioned for her to walk in ahead of him. "We need to press Randall to talk. Last I heard, he was still in the hospital. And we need to find that driver. We have to blow this wide-open—no more keeping the information within the unit. We can't worry about who's involved and who knows what we know. The pictures from the emails on that cell phone have to go wide dispersal."

Jessica looked back at him, squinting against the sun behind his head. "First, we send them to my battalion overseas. It's possible this hasn't gone any further." For the first time, Jessica thought to pray. *Please, Lord, stop this in time.* They might not know what was happening, but Someone else did.

A chair scraped across the floor and Jessica pulled away from Sean. She'd forgotten Staff Duty sitting at the desk.

Private Meyers came around the desk. "Anything I can do for you?"

Jessica eyed him, trying to remember how much she'd said after Sean opened the door. Hopefully not enough to tip off the young soldier that anything was out of the ordinary. "No, thank you. Just going to link back up with Major Braden."

Meyers stepped back and dropped into his chair to stare out the door again, probably bored out of his skull.

Sean pressed a hand into Jessica's lower back, urging her up the hallway. He dropped his voice as they walked. "I'll call Ethan. He can get us clearance to start searching files, see if Ashley can get into the system and find a way to narrow down our orphans and soldiers without close family. I'm not sure if she can, but it's a start."

"The system." Jessica grabbed his arm as they neared her office. "How did they hack the system?"

"It's been done before. The bigger question is, why steal the laptops from a battalion? What was the point? It only called attention to themselves and gained them nothing."

"And why hack my desktop?"

Sean stopped walking and snapped his fingers. "That's it. That's how we narrow down which units they've infiltrated."

"The laptops." Jessica breathed in her first deep breath since the major's call that morning. "We find the units who have reported stolen machines."

Sean's pace quickened as he turned toward the company building. "My computer's in your office and it's definitely not been hacked. Not this time. We need to get those photos to Major Braden and push them overseas. This time, I'm a step ahead of them. This time, I win."

The words tore at her. *This time, I win.* This was Sean's personal vendetta, his score to settle with the men who'd pushed him to the brink. *God, I don't know if this is a good thing or a bad thing. But let him find healing. And keep us all safe.* She reached for him, rushing to catch up with him. "Sean. Wait. This isn't about you."

He spun back to her, fire in his eyes. "It is." He jerked away. "This is all about me. They came after me. They came after Ashley because of me. And they came after you because of me. They don't get to win this round and take you away from me." He turned and was off again before she could respond.

She wanted to dwell on his words but didn't, setting off in pursuit again. There was too much at stake for her feelings to get in the way right now. Too many lives could be in danger. "They'll accelerate whatever their plan is if they know we've figured this out."

"I know. But it will also flush them out into the open. It's a risk we have to take." Sean slowed as he stepped through the door into the building, his mouth a grim line. "We aren't going to keep their secret for them."

Jessica laid a hand on his arm. If she lost him now be-

cause he let the situation drive itself too close to home…
"Don't let this consume you."

He pulled his hand from her arm, expression darkening. "I'm not. I never have. And you don't get to express an opinion when you have no idea what you're talking about." He turned away and stalked toward the door, back rigid. "Grab my laptop and your things and we'll go talk to Major Braden. I'll be in the courtyard."

Jessica slumped against her desk. She was losing him.

No. He was losing himself. Finding a spot on the map to point toward had shifted Sean into high gear in a dangerous direction. Somehow, that scared her more than the idea of impostors infiltrating the ranks. They had the tools at their disposal to deal with the physical threat. It was possible Sean might not survive the spiritual one.

And she couldn't be the one to save him. She had no words. She just turned her prayers toward heaven and let her heart cry out.

But not for long. There was too much to do to stand still. She'd have to put feet to her faith and get moving if they were going to stop anyone else from dying. Leaning across her desk, Jessica reached for the jacket slung over the back of her chair, fingers brushing the black fleece.

The explosion drove Jessica flat against the top of the desk, hands flying to cover her head as the windows shattered. Glass fell in a macabre rain against the tile floor. The blast echoed in the room and in her chest, setting off a ringing in her ears that defied description, just like the concussion of an IED.

Of an IED.

Jessica scrambled off the desk, running her hands across her head and down the front of her plaid shirt. No blood. No pain. She was okay. Her breath stuttered back heavily, pulling her chest in and out until she had to fight her reflexes to get rhythm. *I'm okay. I'm okay.*

But where was Sean? And where was Major Braden?

She bolted for her office door, stopping to listen for footfalls or voices, but the roar in her ears drowned out the whole world. She sensed more than heard the presence beside her and whipped around.

Major Braden and Private Meyers burst through the doors into the company. The major surveyed her. "Are you okay, Staff Sergeant?" His voice sounded as though he spoke through muddy water.

She nodded and swallowed hard, trying to pop her ears, anything to amplify sound. Nothing worked.

Major Braden pointed toward the door. "Meyers, go back to headquarters. Call this in and get emergency here."

Not waiting to see if he'd issue her an order that would slow her down, Jessica ran up the hallway for the door, heart pounding, heedless of anything that might be happening at the end. She had to know Sean hadn't been involved in that blast.

Light shifted at the end of the short hall, and Sean rounded the corner, skidding Jessica to a stop. She pressed a hand against her chest to stop her heart from pounding. "You're okay." She wanted to throw herself at him, prove to herself he wasn't a figment of her imagination, but she held herself in check. Even out of uniform, she wasn't going to cross that line in front of the major.

Sean's gaze scanned her and said he was thinking the same thing. He looked over her head at Major Braden, who'd stopped behind her. "Sir, that was my vehicle in the parking lot."

Jessica took a step back, her elbow colliding with the major's arm. "What?"

"I was in the courtyard, so the building shielded me, but I saw the aftermath." Sean shook his head. "It was mine."

Jessica wanted to sink to the floor. What if they hadn't come back inside? What if they'd gone straight to his vehicle to leave? She held a hand out to Sean, then dropped it to her side. They'd both be dead.

Private Meyers trotted back to them. "Fire and police are on the way."

Sean turned to Jessica. "Go back to your office and stay there until we can get you somewhere safe."

"Me?" She bucked. No way was he going to issue her any sort of directive, not now, not with a blast meant for them still ringing in her ears. "I'm not the target here, and you know it."

"As long as I'm in the picture, both of us are."

Her jaw drew so tight the pain pounded in her ears. "My office has no windows."

Sean scanned her from head to foot again, probably trying to reassure himself that she was all in one piece, but then his expression shifted into neutral. "Find a place. A safe place. I'm going out to meet with emergency and find out what's going on. You fill in Major Braden and get the ball rolling on what we talked about, and then I'll get you out of here."

Jessica dug her fingernails into her palm. Sean was right. Even in the chaos, someone had to move forward with pushing that intel overseas. She turned to the major. "If that's okay with you, I need to grab something from my office, and then we have some things that need to be discussed immediately." She cast a sideways glance at Private Meyers, unwilling to say more in front of anyone who didn't need to know.

Major Braden nodded. "Agreed. My office, Dylan."

Fighting the urge to panic, Jessica headed for her office as he exited the building with the commander. Grabbing Sean's backpack from its place beside her desk, she stopped frozen as the metal blinds clanked together in the chilled breeze. Around the corner, smoke billowed thick from the parking lot.

She tried to swallow but couldn't. How close had they come to being nothing but smoke?

She'd never had a panic attack in her entire life, but her pounding heart and the heat of her skin said there was a first time for everything.

A light tap at her door sent her nearly out of her mind. She whipped around ready to fight.

Private Meyers stood in the doorway, in the process of taking a step back from her wild turn. "Um, Staff Sergeant? The major sent me to get you. He's moved to the conference room."

At the back of the headquarters building. Tucked away from the chaos. It made sense. Jessica hefted the backpack and let Private Meyers usher her out the door.

SIXTEEN

Smoke billowed over the building and dissipated into the wind as onlookers gathered on the perimeter of the parking lot. Sean looked back at the corner of the building around which Jessica's office sat. He couldn't see her windows from here, but if the blast had knocked them out, it was rougher than he'd thought.

In all his life, Sean had never wanted to touch another person as much as he'd wanted to when he saw Jessica in that hallway. With her office on the corner of the building closest to the parking lot, he'd been horrified at what he might see when he found her.

But there she'd stood, safe and whole. He'd wanted to pull her close and shield her from whatever came next. If their targets were going to be brazen enough to blow up a car on a military post, then what came next might be unthinkable.

Which meant he had to do the unthinkable.

Pulling his phone from his pocket, he punched Tate's number.

"Yeah?" Tate's groggy voice came through on the second ring. Even asleep, he was vigilant.

Sean wished he could say the same for himself. They'd rigged his car and he'd missed it, the same way he'd missed them sneaking up to the back of the house. Somehow, he'd lost focus again. "Tate. I'm at the company. I need you to come and get Jessica and get her to headquarters."

"Virginia?" There was a rustle on the line, then Tate's voice, strong and clear. "What happened?"

"They blew my car."

"Whoa."

"She's not safe here, Tate. This is Mina's people and they've just proven they'll do whatever it takes to move this thing forward."

"And to pay you back."

Sean gripped the phone tighter. That discussion wasn't up for grabs right now. If Tate decided Sean was in danger, he'd go over his head to Ethan, who'd order Sean back to Virginia right alongside Jessica. He couldn't risk that. This was their ground zero, and he had to stay and fight. "Jessica's with Major Braden in his office. They're disseminating the photos overseas." He ran down their suspicions to Tate as sirens sounded in the distance. "There's a back door to the building. Use it. We don't need your cover blown. Call me when you're away with her."

"Got it. And watch your back." Tate was gone before Sean could answer, but at least the older man hadn't called Ethan.

Yet.

Sean stayed out of the way as fire trucks swarmed in and firemen dealt with the fire, waiting for Criminal Investigations to show up. The last thing he needed was for the MPs to herd him off the scene with the crowd by the road.

When his phone rang, he stepped back into the relative silence of the courtyard and glanced at the screen.

Tate. There was no way he had Jessica already. It had only been a few minutes since they hung up. If Tate had called Ethan on him, he'd better be ready to fight. "Where are you?"

"Easy, man." Tate's low voice held veiled amusement despite the situation. "I'm nearly there. Just wanted you to know I got a phone call from a buddy of mine. They pulled a body from the river."

"Yeah. The fake Channing."

"Uh-uh. Another one. This time it's a male, found about thirty yards from the first body. I'm going to make an educated guess it's the guy driving your getaway car Monday."

"You think?" Sean couldn't keep the sarcasm out of his voice. "Somebody's running scared, killing off their cohorts. That makes whoever's running this game dangerous." *And more likely to make a mistake.*

"Which makes me think…"

Sean peeked around the corner of the building at the chaos in the parking lot. "Fire away."

"Why blow the car without you in it? If your ringleader isn't above doing away with his own people, he's not going to be kind to you."

"Could've been any number of reasons. A faulty timer. A bad switch. They likely meant it to blow when we started it or had a tilt fuse for when we were driving and it malfunctioned." Maybe Jessica was right. Maybe God was watching out for them.

"Or it's a diversion."

The words sank into Sean's chest. "From what?" He backed up two more steps into the courtyard so he could see the main entrance to the company, dread chasing Tate's words.

"I'm just thinking it's a little odd the thing went off right after you put two and two together."

"I hear you, but there was only a couple of minutes of lag time between us putting the pieces together and then deciding to leave." The dread burrowed deeper. Something wasn't right. It dug at his subconscious and refused to lock in. He took two more steps toward the building.

"It could have been there awhile while they waited for the opportune time."

"Why not just set it off and kill us when they could?"

"Revenge," Tate said. "You said it yourself. They've got a need to hurt you. Anybody hear you talking?"

A diversion. A need to hurt you. "Only person who could have heard anything we said was…Meyers. The private at staff duty." Sean broke into a run. That was the thing that had been nagging him. Meyers was off his post when Channing broke into Jessica's office, and he was back in again pulling staff duty three days later? He'd been right there when they walked into the building. And he hadn't been at his post when Sean stepped outside to wait for Jessica just before the car went up. "That's why he seemed familiar. His picture must have been on the cell phone, and Jessica never made it through all of the pictures. We missed him. He's in on it."

Sean burst through the doors to the battalion, praying Meyers would be sitting there, but the desk was empty. The staff duty officer was outside, so where was Meyers? He shoved his phone into his pocket and barreled past the desk toward the major's office. He pushed into the room without knocking, the door only opening about three-quarters of the way before it hit resistance. Sean edged around the door.

Major Braden lay on the floor, neck at an odd angle,

lips already turning blue. Sean ducked down to feel for a pulse. Nothing but rapidly cooling skin, no movement.

Sick dread choked him as he backed away from the body and scanned the room. Jessica's phone lay on the desk.

"Jessica!" Doubling back up the hallway, Sean checked each area of the headquarters building. Empty.

He bolted back through the lobby, slowing to a stop in front of the staff duty desk. His laptop sat in the center of the table, opened to face him, the screen saver scrolling the time. Had it only been fifteen minutes since he left her?

He reached for the machine when his phone vibrated in his pocket. *Please be Jessica.*

No. Ashley. He jerked the phone to his ear, words already racing with his thoughts. "Dig into a soldier in Jessica's battalion. A Private Meyers. He's got Jessica."

"I know." Her voice was tense in a way he hadn't heard since shortly after he'd been abducted himself.

"How?"

"Check your email. They're playing our game against us."

Grabbing his laptop, he ducked back up the hall to the small conference room and logged on. "What am I looking for?"

"They sent me a message from your secure email."

Sean's fingers froze on the keys. "How did they get into that?" Those accounts were buried deep. Access required two different encrypted passwords.

Ashley didn't answer.

"Tell me." Sean ground the words out as he logged into his account. One new email waited in his inbox, sent from his own address. Bile rose and he swallowed hard.

"They hacked me." Again. He pounded his hand on the table. Somehow, he'd failed again.

"I'll figure it out. But I don't think it's on your end."

It didn't matter. He'd still failed Jessica. He clicked the link and scanned the email.

Where was your post office box?

"They're taunting me about the last op?" It was childish, foolish. He clicked on the attachment and found an image of his burning vehicle, then noticed the file size. It was too big to be a simple picture.

The photo. The question. His fingers went numb. "They have our program." The same program that had blown Mina's terror cell apart was being used against them. Sean had encoded intelligence inside photos and sent them back to a post office box in Black River, New York for Ashley to decipher using software they'd developed together during her recovery.

"How would they get it?"

"I don't know." Sean closed his eyes, pulled in air and opened the program he'd buried in his hard drive, then clicked on the photo. A small box popped up and he typed the words. *Black River.*

A second photo popped open on the screen and Sean's stomach twisted and threatened to make a run up for air.

A close-up of Jessica. Bound…a knife at her throat.

No matter how hard Jessica swallowed… No matter how hard she tried to think of something else… Nothing could take away the feel of the cold blade that had pressed against her throat. She wanted to claw at the spot until some other, harsher sensation wiped it away but she couldn't. Her hands were duct taped behind her, pressed into the fabric of the front bucket seat in Meyers's truck.

They pulled closer to the guard gate to exit post and Jessica tried to hold her breath steady. Maybe if she screamed, they'd hear her.

Meyers seemed to read her thoughts. "I meant what I said. You do anything to indicate you're in trouble, I'll kill you and anyone who tries to rescue you. While it would be a whole lot more poetic for Turner to watch you die, I can handle it if he only gets to grieve the fact he couldn't save you."

Jessica's eyes drifted shut. She was going to die either way, but the choice of whether to take down an innocent gate guard with her... At least this way, she bought time. How much, she had no idea.

She fought the duct tape holding her hands and only succeeded in having it cut into her skin. She was trapped. She had nothing sharp to cut with, couldn't unfasten her seat belt and lunge across the console to wreck the vehicle—she was along for the ride, wherever Meyers decided to take her. She fought to keep herself from panic. "Where are we going?"

He smiled ever so slightly. "Your house."

"Why?" She clamped her mouth shut. Tate was at the house. If Meyers took her there, she had an ally he knew nothing about. If only she could get a message to Tate that she needed help before he walked out of his makeshift bedroom into something he was totally unprepared for.

"It's home base. Sooner or later, Turner will show up. We'll just wait until he does."

As they passed through the gate headed off post, Jessica tried to gain the attention of someone—anyone—but there was no way. Meyers had chosen Gate 7, the one with the farthest distance between the entrance and exit roads. Even if a guard did turn toward her, he'd likely never be able to read her desperation.

And she had no doubt Meyers would slash her throat before help could get to her. She slumped against the seat, head down, not willing to make eye contact with the driver of the car beside them at the stoplight. It was too risky, too many lives at stake.

Lord... What should she pray anyway? That Sean figured out what was going on and found her quickly? That would only land both of them in danger. That Tate was awake and alert at the house? That would only get him killed if Meyers surprised him. *Lord, whatever needs to happen. Just get us out of this alive.* She couldn't think of anything else, just let her heart cry out in desperation she couldn't even begin to express.

As her pulse slowed to normal, she lifted her head and dared to take in their surroundings. He was headed for the highway, which meant he'd likely take Wilma Rudolph into downtown. Normally, it would be the most crowded route, but on Thanksgiving Day? The boulevard would be a virtual dead zone. If she could only work her fingers to the side and hit the seat belt buckle... But she'd never get back around to the door fast enough to open it and dive out before Meyers was on to her. Until he got her out of the truck at her house, all she could do was wait.

And make him talk. "Why do this? You took an oath to protect..." She sat back farther in the seat. The fake soldiers. "You're not Private Meyers."

"I'm not even a soldier, but I read a whole lot of books about them." He smiled. "You can call me Joel. The real Private Meyers is peacefully sleeping in some woods outside of Fort Benning, Georgia. I met him at a bar. Poor guy had no family to miss him, just a girlfriend he broke up with over email when he moved up here to Campbell. So sad." He said it so matter-of-factly, so casually, as if life was disposable, easily dismissed.

Jessica tugged at the duct tape again, but it held tight. He would kill her and Sean and Tate and anyone else who got in his way if he needed to. She had no more doubts.

"Why?"

"Why ask the question?" Joel flicked a hard, dark gaze her way. "You and Turner already figured it out. I did hear you talking, you know. Neither of you has a quiet voice." He chuckled. "Too bad, too. You could be headed home to make your turkey or whatever it is you were going to make today if you'd just given me twenty-four more hours. Then it wouldn't matter who you told. It would all be in motion."

"Whoever is pulling the strings on this thing was going to make it seem like soldiers turned on soldiers. Make teams mistrust each other."

"Make them wonder who was going to pull the trigger next. Just a couple…every day…over time. Until nobody can even rest their heads on their pillows over here or over there because you just never know who's going to wield the weapon next."

Jessica wanted to ram a fist into his smug mouth. The idea that her brothers and sisters could be slaughtered by ones they perceived to be their own, could view each other with distrust, could be so afraid for their lives in places that should be safe… The fire that blew through her had nothing to do with fear. "How many?"

He chuckled. "You'd love it if I told you. But I can tell you this." He winked. "I'm the one in charge. Your battalion is my baby."

"How many?" She barely knew the men and women

who'd crossed over with her brigade, but she'd spoken to parents, to spouses, to friends…

He waved a hand in the air and wiggled his fingers. "Guess."

She bit her tongue. No way would she give him the satisfaction. "Why?"

"Because it's what my father wanted."

The familiar sentiment, coming from the mouth of a killer, chilled her blood. How many times had she thought the same thing, turned her life a different direction because of her father? And here sat a murderer, citing the same reason. Maybe it was a common link she could manipulate, gain some sympathy, make him see her as human. She tried to steady her voice, gall rising at the idea of trying to connect with the man beside her. "I understand."

"Really." The word drew out on a wave of skepticism.

"My father wants me to be an officer. To be like him and my brother. Only problem is, I never quite measured up." And she never would. She could become an officer, but it still wouldn't be good enough. Never. There would only be more to measure up to. Why did she have to be staring down death to see that?

"My father isn't forcing me to do anything. I'm just taking over the family business."

Jessica couldn't do it anymore. Couldn't pretend to sympathize with the man beside her. "Your father's a terrorist?"

His hand flew across the space between them, his knuckle driving her lip against her teeth. "He's a fighter against your country's tyranny."

Jessica held her head steady and blinked back tears as blood oozed metallic behind her teeth. She ran her tongue along the inside of her damaged lip, trying not to wince. "Our tyranny?"

"Your nose is everywhere it shouldn't be, your fighters marching for freedom. Well, not every person on earth deserves freedom. Not every person on earth is equal. In the end, someone has to be the most powerful and rule the others. And my father was helping to make that happen."

She wanted to plug her ears to keep from hearing any more. Scream at the top of her lungs to let out the tension. Anything but sit here with her insides feeling as if they were going to push out of her skin more with every word Meyers spoke.

As he turned on to her street, Jessica found her driveway. Tate's car was missing.

Her last hope plummeted. She'd be in an empty house with a man bent on hurting Sean through her. A man willing to harm her and take photographic evidence that would torture Sean for life. Her heart hammered harder and she swallowed a rush of panic. If she lost control, she'd never be able to escape if the opportunity arose.

She scanned her neighbors' yards. Most were empty in the late-morning laziness of Thanksgiving Day, but several houses down and across the street, a small cluster of teenage boys tossed a football.

When she turned away, Joel was watching her as he slowed in front of her house. He cast a pointed glance at the boys but said nothing.

He didn't have to.

She turned away, unable to stomach the message he was communicating. *Please, God. No more death.* Let the neighbors all stay inside their warm houses, clueless to what was about to happen inside her own. At the moment, that was her greatest prayer.

But movement a few doors down caught her eye as Major White walked out of his house, seemed to catch sight of the truck, and stepped off his porch with purpose. She prayed Joel didn't notice.

But he did. "Is he coming this way?"

Jessica stiffened. "Probably." Why lie? His destination would be clear in two seconds anyway.

"You will not tell him anything, and you already know why."

Jessica whipped toward him, sick of the threat. "I know why. You'll kill me. You'll kill him. You'll blow up the world. Got it." She turned her back on him and stuck her arms between them. "But he's going to know something's wrong the minute he sees me when my hands don't come out from behind my back at all." She spit the words out like acid, anger heating the cab of the truck.

Joel's face hardened, then he pulled out his knife. "Turn around. But I assure you, I'll use this if you so much as trip over a tree root."

"Got it." She bit off the words and pulled the sleeves of her plaid shirt down over her wrists, then pushed the truck door open.

"Jessica." Retired Major Dan White crossed the next-door neighbor's yard, his step sure, his bearing projecting his military status to anyone in his presence. "I heard from your father a little bit ago. He's been trying to call your cell phone."

"I had to go into work. I must have left it there." Her mind raced around the words, trying to find some way to communicate with her neighbor.

Joel stepped up beside her, drawing the major's attention before he looked back at Jessica with an arched eyebrow.

Now. Now was the time to ask for help. Hoping her

voice didn't betray her, she lifted her hand and brushed a loose piece of hair behind her ear, letting the sleeve of her shirt fall below her wrist. She kept her gaze hard on the major's, flicking a glance to her wrist only once, praying he'd hear what she wasn't saying. "I'll have Sean here take me back to get it in a few minutes."

Joel laid a hand on her back and extended his free hand. "Sean Turner. Nice to meet you, sir."

The major shook his hand and never turned back to Jessica. "You, as well. Make sure she calls her father, Sean. And you two have a nice Thanksgiving."

The major turned and walked back to his house.

Joel pressed her back. "Let's go."

Jessica tried not to let her posture slump. Her last chance at rescue was walking away.

SEVENTEEN

Sean pounded his palm on the desk in Jessica's office at the company. When the MPs took over the battalion headquarters, he'd cleared his presence with them and moved to his own base of operations. He had to find Jessica, and while the MPs had locked down post as soon as he told them her situation, there was no way they'd stopped Meyers if he was already past the gate.

And now his chain of command had lost their minds. "I am not going to get on a helicopter and fly back to Virginia. No." He flicked his finger across the track pad of his laptop and leaned closer to the computer, searching for a clue to where Jessica was. Anything to get him moving closer and not away from her to Virginia.

Ethan's voice poured out of the speaker on Sean's phone, stationed on Jessica's desk, filling the room with its authority. "Commander's about to order it."

There was no way they could expect him to get on a helicopter and take shelter in a secure location when Jessica was in danger. It violated everything. "Ethan, you can't expect me to follow that order. When you had Ashley with you and she was in danger, would you have just taken off and left her to whoever they decided could search for her? In that moment when Mitch had her, would you have backed off and turned the reins over to someone else?"

Tate reached over and laid a hand on Sean's shoulder, probably trying to reel him in. It had been Tate's home that was shot up during Ethan and Ashley's escape from Sam Mina's men. Tate's cover that was blown so he had no safe place to land even now, seven months later. Yet here he stood, by Sean's side, his peace almost palpable.

Even Tate Walker's unflappable presence wasn't helping Sean right now. He was too close to going over the edge. Everything was out of control. Everything. Why couldn't God let one thing go his way, especially when Jessica's life was on the line?

The phone crackled, a sure indication Ethan was on a secure channel. "Listen to my words carefully. The commander is *about* to order it."

Sean froze. Was he saying—?

"Lose your phone, buddy." Tate reached over and took the device from Sean's hand, cutting the call then holding the phone out to Sean. "Kincaid just gave you a heads-up. You can't follow an order you never receive."

"He's going to get us both called on the carpet for insubordination." The wry words covered up Sean's swirling emotions as he shoved his phone into his hip pocket. Jessica was out there somewhere, and he had no idea where. All he could do was stand in her office and stare at the horrific photo, searching for a clue. Sitting still was about to kill him, but running off half-cocked for parts unknown would be worse.

She'd been in the headquarters building, only feet away when Meyers took her, and Sean hadn't been fast enough. He'd missed her, and now… She could be anywhere. On post. Off post. On a plane somewhere halfway to the other side of the world. He dug his fingers into his thigh. The clock was ticking and he was out of options. Nowhere to turn. No more control.

Seems to me you're relying a whole lot on Sean Turner and not nearly enough on God. Jessica's words from last night swirled in the chaos of his mind. Last night. Only last night? It felt like weeks ago. If he could pull her close again, he'd listen. He wouldn't push her away.

He wouldn't let her go.

Lord, I don't know where she is, but You do. I can't keep her safe, but You can. There was no flash of knowledge, no sudden vision of Jessica's whereabouts, but the fringes of peace settled in. Jessica was right. God had rescued him, had saved Ashley, had given him a family... Now he was at the end of himself and could only trust this would all work out.

"Where is she, Tate?" The words bore an anguish he never let anyone else hear. Ever.

Tate blew out a loud sigh. "I don't know. It was fifteen minutes from the time you left her until you figured out she was gone. She could have been gone fourteen of those minutes or two."

"He had time to get off post before the MPs locked it down, though." And that made their search infinitely harder.

"And you can't just drive around aimlessly. That's a waste of energy. As soon as the MPs get the info about his vehicle registration, they'll put out a BOLO for him. He's taunting you. He'll contact you again. Best thing for you to do is pull up your email and wait."

It might be the best thing, but it was the last thing Sean wanted. He swiped the track pad again, but his inbox still sat empty, the huge blank space mocking him more than the man who'd taken Jessica ever could. No news. None.

Flipping back to the picture, he focused on the background, the dark edges. Anything but Jessica's face and the tension that lodged there.

His cell phone vibrated in his pocket. "Somebody's calling."

"Your call whether to answer it," Tate said. "You hear the order and you're at the airfield on the next helicopter out. No excuses."

Sean tapped his thumb on the track pad, then pulled his phone from his pocket. He'd never violated a direct order, and the decision whether to evade now weighed on him. Jessica? Or his integrity?

But the area code was 931. A Clarksville exchange. He held the phone up to show Tate, then took the call against his better judgment. "Hello?"

"Staff Sergeant Turner?" The voice was unfamiliar but heavy with authority.

Had the commander figured out Ethan had tipped him off and had someone else call him? Surely not. "Yes, sir."

"This is Dan White. We met the other night at Jessica Dylan's house."

Sean stood. What did Jessica's neighbor want? He didn't have time for petty issues. "Yes, sir. Can I help you?"

"You asked me to call you if I noticed anything down at Jessica Dylan's house, and I'm going to guess a man pretending to be you qualifies."

His heart pounded faster. Something was up. He motioned for Tate to move out and grabbed his laptop. "A man pretending to be me, sir? He's at Jessica's?"

"Jessica's at the house with a man claiming to be you. And here's another thing… Her wrists look like she's gone three rounds with some razor wire. What's going on, Staff Sergeant?"

Thank You, Lord. Jessica was at her house. She was

still in danger, but he was no longer at the mercy of terrorists. He knew where she was. Sean caught up to Tate as they stepped onto the quad. "Jessica's house. Now. He's holding her there. Call the MPs and tell them to let the gate know we're coming through."

"Turner?" Major White grew gruffer.

"Sir, don't go back to the house. That man kidnapped Jessica from her battalion. Keep an eye on the place and let me know if they leave, but do not approach. We're on the way."

"Police?"

If the police roared up with sirens blaring and a hostage negotiator at the ready, Meyers would switch up the plan and kill Jessica immediately. They needed more stealth. An FBI hostage rescue team would take too long. But surely Ethan could call in some favors from his Special Forces buddies. "Call Captain Ethan Kincaid." He rattled off Ethan's secure cell number. "Tell him I told you to call and then tell him everything you told me. Tell him to pull in every favor he's ever been owed. He'll get bigger guns than the police into place faster than they can."

There was a stretch of silence. "How do I know I can trust you, Turner?"

"Because I need Jessica to be safe." He couldn't put it into words, the emotion was too big. But the Major had to hear it.

"I'm making the call. And don't do anything stupid, Turner. God's got a better hold on her than any man ever could."

Sean ended the call, the major's words washing him in a peace that he really shouldn't be feeling given the situation. He cleared his throat as he slid into Tate's car. "Guy talks like you do."

"Then he's a genius. Maybe you should listen."

Sean held on to his laptop with his free hand as Tate blew through a yellow light and aimed for Gate 4 at a speed just barely above legal. If Sean had his way, they'd be blowing through town with a police tail trying to catch them. As they edged around angry drivers waiting to leave post through heightened security, he leaned forward as if the extra inches would gain Jessica time.

Sean leaned across Tate and flashed his ID, getting a wave-through that likely frustrated every driver in line, then tried to settle back into his seat and plan their next move.

The phone vibrated in his hand once, then stopped. A text. He pulled the device out and wanted to peek at it through hooded lids so he couldn't see it if the commander had uncharacteristically decided to text an order. They knew where Jessica was. They were too close to saving her for him to pull back now.

The screen displayed Ashley's number.

Meyers is Joel Mina. Sam's son.

Sean's breath caught like a punch to the chest. This wasn't a simple revenge plot. It was worse. This was personal. Ugly. His core iced over. Sam Mina's men had nearly destroyed Sean for nothing more than gathering intel on them. If his son had Jessica and was intent on inflicting pain on Sean through her to avenge his father's imprisonment, even Sean's worst nightmares couldn't conjure up what the man would do to destroy them both.

EIGHTEEN

The house was milky dark in the midmorning light, the curtains still closed from the night before. The sun shone through the branches of the oak tree in the front yard, casting dancing shadows on the fabric. The rest of the house stood silent and empty with Angie at her parents' and Tate vanished. Likely, after the car bomb, he was right back where she'd just left, by Sean's side. She just prayed Joel hadn't laid any traps for them.

She prayed they were safe and Ashley had distributed photos out in time to stop whatever Joel's master plan was. She could almost handle death if it meant others survived. Sacrificing herself for the good of the nation might finally make her father proud. She rolled her eyes. What a thought for such a moment. She must be losing her grip on her sanity.

Joel shoved her into the entryway and shut the door. He eyed her with calculated intent as he fingered the straps of the gray backpack he'd slung over his shoulder.

He must have slipped the knife in there when he saw Major White coming. She didn't even want to think about what else he might have concealed in its depths.

Now was her moment. She was unfettered, and while his knife wasn't at the ready, she had one chance to break away and run, to save herself and Sean. She took one step back and judged the distance to the side door.

He followed her gaze, then shook his head, that hard expression still in his eye. "I get what you're thinking, but let me assure you of something. Run, and I don't bother chasing you first." He looked behind him in the direction of the kids playing football. "They'll never see me coming."

He had her there. Even if she muscled past him and burst out the front door screaming his intent, it would only bring people running into danger. He could still harm someone else before he was taken down. Whatever he had in mind, it was highly likely he wasn't afraid of dying to make his point.

Running might not be the answer, but coming at him with her full strength could be. He was taller and broader than her. Did she dare take that chance? If she caught him by surprise, she might be able to take him down, but if she didn't succeed the first time...

A chance at taking him to his knees was better than the certainty of being restrained and tortured while she waited for him to kill Sean. The way he'd taunted Sean with that photo of her taken at the battalion, she had no doubt what was coming next. The cold of that knife still lay heavy against her throat, but she refused to give him the satisfaction of seeing her try to wipe the sensation away.

She took a step back, sweeping the small living room for anything that could be used as a weapon. Blankets lay balled at the end of the couch where Sean had slept. *Where Sean slept.* His pistol was always at his side, within easy reach whenever he bunked down for the night. It was close at hand wherever they went... except on post. He had no authorization to carry it on Fort

Campbell and she couldn't remember him stowing it in the rental car this morning, so it had to be in the house somewhere. The problem was, she had no idea where he secured it when he didn't need it. With his gear scattered around her living room, it couldn't possibly be far. She just didn't have any way to search for it.

No, a full-on physical confrontation was the only chance she had, and she'd have to take it soon, before Joel had her bound again. Until then, she had to keep him talking, keep his mind off his plan and slow him down. "What are you going to do?" There seemed to be some weakness, some anger there. Maybe it would pull his emotions up and dull his edge.

"Make Sean Turner suffer." The cold, hard hatred in the words took away every thought of appealing to his reason. Joel had an agenda that went past anything Jessica could talk him down from. This was more than a terror threat. It was a personal vendetta. He jerked his head toward the open dining room at the back of the house and hitched the backpack higher. "Let's go."

Jessica stood defiant. She might not be able to appeal to his sense of reason, but she could play on every other emotion he had. "What's he ever done to you?"

His gaze came back to hers, colder than any she'd ever seen. "Because of my father. He was going to turn the tide of this war until Turner and his friends decided a warrior is better off in prison. Now it falls to me, but only after I make Turner and his friends pay."

Sean was responsible for Joel's father being in jail. That could only mean... Jessica's jaw slackened. His father headed the terror cell Sean had helped bring down when he was in Afghanistan, the one Ashley and her husband had helped bring to justice. What was that name he'd said, the one he'd been convinced would come after him? "You're Sam Mina's son."

"You know the name?" Joel smiled again, this time with some sort of prideful satisfaction. "So Turner has talked about him. I guess my father and his men made an impression after all."

"A very, very little."

Joel's face darkened, and he took two steps closer to her, his fists tensed as if he planned to strike. "Well, it's about to be very, very big. Turner went into hiding after he was rescued and my father was arrested, but my people and I figured we could flush him or his partner Kincaid out if we played our cards right. And we did. The fact that their secret little military unit sent Turner instead of Kincaid is a bonus I can only be very grateful for."

"How?" He was talking. She had to keep it that way.

"The laptops. Although you figured it out more quickly than I'd planned and forced me to speed up the timeline. By stealing the laptops, I established a puzzle with no answer. I didn't need them. But by taking them twice, and then letting a little bit of chatter out about the next one, it drew the unit Turner is involved in out into the open."

Jessica wanted to sink to the floor in defeat. That was why the laptop thefts had never fit in, why the puzzle pieces didn't match. Sam Mina's son was a genius. An unhinged, sociopathic genius.

"I didn't even need the back door Specialist Channing opened on your desktop."

Channing. "What was her real name?"

"I have no idea. My part was to run the technology, to create the hack that revealed Turner overseas. My father recruited her and the others and they were already training in military formalities when he was arrested. I just picked up where he left off, leading from the inside. As for your computer, I opened the back door so that Ashley Kincaid would have something to play with, something to focus on while I worked my way back through her open channel. While she was busy on your computer, I was busy on hers."

That was the program that Ashley couldn't identify on her computer. While they thought they were winning, Joel Mina was tearing them apart.

Jessica wanted to sink to the floor. Everything they thought they knew, everything they thought was true, was an upside-down lie, a fabrication by a man who'd thought things out six steps ahead of them.

"I purposely left my signature in that code so she'd know she's not the best there is, that someone can step in and overwrite everything she's done." He straightened his posture. "I developed the hack that let us change up the photos in the ID card database so my people could get new cards."

Keep talking. His arrogance was showing, bleeding through, taking his focus off her and laying it on his own accomplishments. If he'd only look away… Jessica tensed her legs, ready to spring the moment he turned his attention away from her.

He smiled, self-satisfied and smug. "She and Turner thought their little program was untouchable. But it's not. I have it now. And I can sell it to the highest bidder as soon as we're all finished here. On the open market, with a few tweaks, that kind of encryption could be—"

Jessica bent her knees and sprang at him, her shoulder catching Joel in the chest and driving him backward toward the door.

His feet tangled under him, and he landed with a grunt, half on his back and half propped into the door.

Scrambling back, Jessica jerked her arm back and threw a solid blow to his jaw, driving his head back hard against the door. Shaking off the pain to her knuckles, she pulled back to throw another punch, but at the farthest point back, Joel threw his arm out, his hand catching the side of her neck and throwing her sideways. He rolled with the momentum, pinning her facedown beneath him.

Grinding a knee into the small of her back, he bent her arm, jerking her wrist to her neck until her already-injured shoulder threatened to separate. He leaned low, increasing the pressure of his weight on her arm and pulling a whimper from her throat. With his free hand, he pressed her head into the floor, sand and grit digging into her cheek. "I warned you." His voice was loud against her ear. He eased the pressure slightly.

Jessica lifted her head, fighting to keep her wits against the pain in her shoulder, searching for leverage to throw him off her back.

As soon as her head lifted, Joel slammed it into the floor, slinging shooting lights across her vision.

Her temple pounded and her vision clouded. She hardly felt him move as he leaned to the side and pulled the backpack closer. Pinning her with his knee, he freed his hand to unzip the backpack and retrieve the roll of duct tape. "You just made hurting you a whole lot easier."

It took everything Sean had not to shove Tate out of the way and slam the pedal of the sedan all the way to the floor. If the cops followed him, it was more firepower to the party.

Firepower. "Are you armed?" Since he couldn't carry

it on post, Sean had left his pistol in the trunk of the rental car while on Fort Campbell, locked up and unloaded. He assumed it had gone up with the rest of the vehicle.

"Got my Sig in the trunk." Tate negotiated the turn onto Jessica's street at a speed most drivers would consider unsafe and kept his focus on the road. "I'm guessing you're weaponless?"

"At the moment, but I have an idea." Boy, did he hope it panned out. If not, they were going up against a terrorist with a grudge and only one weapon between the two of them.

"How long before Ethan's reinforcements get here?"

"They had to get orders, and the last text I had gave an ETA of half an hour. We haven't got that kind of time." Sean had spent the entire ride with his laptop open, intent on the email icon, praying in a way he hadn't prayed in years that another photo wouldn't show up in his inbox. An incoming email would have stopped his heart, would have been a telltale sign that Joel Mina had already started torturing Jessica. He lifted his head from the screen and pointed to a driveway several houses up from Jessica's. "Pull in there and hide the car behind that SUV."

"This is the nosy neighbor's house?" Tate slowed and negotiated the turn at a more sedate pace, nearly driving Sean to jump out of the vehicle and run the last few yards himself.

"The nosy neighbor who's a retired major in Special Forces." One Sean desperately hoped had a gun or two at the ready.

In spite of the situation, Tate chuckled. "You make the right kinds of friends, Turner." He shifted the car into

Park as Sean threw the door open. "Or God's watching out for you."

There wasn't time to ponder that comment now. Three doors down, Jessica might be fighting for her life.

The side door slipped open, and the major stepped out, waving Sean and Tate forward. He cut an imposing figure, height matching Sean's own six feet, hair not quite as gray as it should be, but streaking back from the temples, leaving silver lines in a sea of brown. "Been keeping an eye on the place. No one's left."

Sean clasped his extended hand. "This is a friend of mine. He's armed, and I'm not. Think you can help a guy out?"

The major flashed a quick smile and jerked a thumb toward the house. "Got you a Glock 20 and a Sig P229 laid out there on the table by the door in case you needed them. Take your pick." As Sean started to pass, the major laid a hand on his arm, all semblance of humor dropping away. "And you don't know how hard it's been not to carry both of them down the street myself."

Sean swallowed the emotion that welled up and threatened to choke him. All he could do was nod. Nobody knew better than him. All he wanted at the moment was to break into a run, weapon or no.

Sean hefted the Glock and checked the chamber, then slid in one magazine and pocketed a second. He caught Tate's eye over the major's shoulder. "You ready for this? I'm not waiting twenty more minutes on Ethan's guys." Not when he had no idea what Joel Mina was doing to Jessica. His imagination was giving him trouble enough. *Lord, get us through this and get us out of there alive.*

Major White lifted the Sig from the small table. "Whatever you're planning, I'm with you."

Sean started to argue, then stopped himself. With the major's training, he likely knew more than Sean and Tate put together.

Sean caught Tate's approval and nodded. "Yes, sir." He stepped out of the shelter of the small carport and looked around the house to Jessica's. Up the street, several boys gathered up a football and headed for their front door. The neighborhood was quiet otherwise.

From the front, Jessica's house stood empty and silent, but there was no telling what waited behind those drawn curtains. Joel Mina might not know they had him figured out yet, or he might be two steps ahead of them and laid every trap imaginable.

Sean tightened his fingers on the Glock's grip and tapped his index finger on the side of the barrel. "We can't all go in the front or we risk a neighbor getting suspicious and investigating or calling the police and escalating this. Tate, take the side door and come in when you hear me call you. Sir, keep an eye on the front door and don't hesitate if you hear something that makes you think we need you. If Ethan's buddies show up early, step away and fill them in. I'm going in the back." He broke away and headed for the backyard to avoid showing himself from the street.

Tate grabbed his elbow as Sean passed. "The major and I will go. You're staying here. You've got too much emotionally invested in this."

"You're out of the Army, Walker." Sean refused to meet Tate's eye and jerked away to continue on his intended path, walking away from a confrontation with his friend. Tate wasn't the enemy, and Sean wasn't going to expend energy or waste time fighting his partner. "You can't give me an order." There was no way he was sitting idly by while someone else put their life on the line for his mistake in Afghanistan.

One way or another, this ended today.

NINETEEN

From the back corner of the small brick house next door, Sean watched Tate take up a position next to Jessica's side door, his back pressed tight against the house. In the front, Major White crept into position, crouched low by the steps and hidden from the street by large azalea bushes.

Tate caught Sean's eye and nodded, pointing with two fingers for Sean to move. The house must be silent or Tate would have signaled otherwise and had them both go in fighting.

Sean wasn't sure if that was a blessing or not.

Staying low, gun at the ready before him, Sean crept between the houses and along the covered porch behind Jessica's, scanning the windows for movement, but the house was still. He slipped up the stairs and across the wood floor, keeping close to the wall. It hadn't even been twelve hours since he'd pushed Jessica away from him on this same porch, had told her God didn't care. Based on everything he'd seen so far today—every clue dropped in their lap at the right moment—he'd been severely wrong on all counts.

And if he ever got Jessica to safety again, he'd tell her every single thing he'd been wrong about, including pushing her and God away in his need to do this all himself. He'd never been more certain than he was right now, on the brink of losing Jessica, that he needed someone else.

And despite the fact he'd only known her a handful of days, he was growing more certain by the minute that it was her.

But none of that mattered if he couldn't get her safely out of that house and neutralize Joel Mina. That was a feat he couldn't do on his own, and now, crouched on her back porch, he knew, with a clarity he'd never known before, whom he needed.

It wasn't just Jessica. He needed the God he'd been shoving away for far too long. The God who'd proven Himself faithful through everything, even when Sean insisted he could do this all by himself.

He couldn't even save himself. It wasn't in his power. Jessica was right in what she said last night. Every step of the way, God had rescued him… Ashley… Ethan… And today He'd led Sean right to Jessica. God wasn't hands-off just because He didn't do things the way Sean wanted. He was fully involved, guiding Sean in spite of every mistake he made.

Sean checked that he was hidden well, then turned his eyes skyward. He could take one minute to do this right. *Okay. I give up, God. This is all Yours. You're the only One who can get us all out of this alive, so I'm handing it over. Right now. All of it. Because I need You to be in charge.*

There was no miraculous rescue. No lightning bolt from the blue that zapped through the house and struck Joel Mina. But there was strength. A new strength that came from letting go. Sean grabbed it and held on, breathing it in, ready to follow God's lead wherever it led.

He slipped Jessica's house key from his pocket and tried to remember if the door leading from the small laundry room to the hallway had been closed this morning. Unless Tate had opened it before he left, his last memory was seeing it tightly shut as he walked up the hallway. Sean said a quick prayer that it still was and slipped the key into the lock.

The key settling into place sounded like a jackhammer to his straining ears, and he clicked the lock slowly, then eased the door open, unable to remember if it squeaked or not. For the first time, he was grateful there was no alarm to signal his entry.

Clearing the laundry room, he stepped to the door leading into the hallway and pressed his ear to the wood. Nothing. No talking. No movement. He was going in blind, with no idea where Joel was holding Jessica. He cataloged the house and eliminated the idea that Joel had taken her upstairs. Too much difficulty, and Jessica was smart enough to throw Joel off balance on the stairs and take him down. No, they had to be downstairs. The only rooms to the right of the laundry room were the bathroom and the office where Tate had been bunking, which left the living and dining room area or the kitchen, both wide-open to the hallway as soon as he stepped out if Joel Mina was standing in the right spot.

Sean would have to take his chances. And pray that Tate and the major were good at kicking in doors.

Readying his trigger finger, Sean pulled the door open and peered around it.

No one stood in his line of sight. Back close to the wall, he crept up the hallway, weapon at the ready.

Just before the hallway opened up, he stopped, listening. A low, guttural series of groans cut the silence. Jessica. He inched nearer and saw her foot, then followed it up. She was bound with duct tape to one of her dining room chairs, a bruise red and angry above the tape covering her mouth.

But she was alive.

A force from the left slammed him forward into the opposite wall, trapping his weapon between him and the hard surface, the corner of the wall crashing into his forearm and shooting lightning bolts clear to his shoulder. He gripped the gun tighter and forced himself backward, using the wall for leverage and driving his attacker back into the living room. They stumbled together, Sean landing on his back on his attacker's legs.

Rolling to the side, he hefted up to level his weapon, but Joel Mina swung his foot, catching Sean in the wrist and sending the gun skittering across the floor.

Rather than dive after the weapon, Sean used his height advantage to throw himself at Joel, catching him at the stomach and driving him backward into the couch, flipping him over the back. Sean lost his footing just before he tumbled over after Mina.

Mina's head crashed into the coffee table and he rolled off the side, landing on his hands and knees.

Rounding the side of the couch, Sean leaped again as Joel tried to stand. Sean caught him in the side and drove him to the ground, pinning him there by his throat with his left hand and driving a fist into his jaw with his right as the side door crashed open behind him. He'd never, ever wanted to kill a man before, but his mind clouded with the image of Jessica bound behind him, bruised and wounded.

"Turner." Tate appeared in his peripheral vision, weapon leveled on Mina. "It's over. Get Jessica."

Sean released Mina, resisting the urge to slam his knuckles into the man's face one more time, and backed away as the major came in the busted side door followed by two heavily armed men in black.

Let them have Mina. He brushed past Tate and went straight to Jessica, seeing nothing else but her, tears of relief leaking down her cheeks and weakening his muscles as the adrenaline ebbed.

He knelt in front of her and blew out the breath he felt he'd been holding for hours, then reached up and pulled the duct tape from her cheek, wincing in sympathy as it pulled away, leaving a red burn in its wake. Pressing the tape into the carpet, he reached up and laid a hand against her uninjured cheek. "You okay?"

"Yeah." She nodded, leaning her palm into his. "Or I will be. Just…get me out of here."

He nodded, not trusting his voice. His surrender outside had unlocked something around his heart, something that kept him from breathing when he was this close to her. He was gone. Done. Finished. In love with this woman in a way that physically ached, that locked his jaw and kept him from speaking the words. He stood, trying to put enough space between them to allow him to speak.

One of the soldiers in black stepped up and held out a knife. "Got a message for you from Captain Kincaid." The man grinned beneath his eye protection and helmet. "Said to tell you guys that they rounded up the impostors in Dylan's battalion and passed the word ahead to the rest. Army's got eyes wide-open and is checking every soldier in the ranks."

Jessica slumped. "We did it." She tipped her head toward Joel Mina, who was being hauled out the door by two more armed men. "We beat him."

Sean knelt behind Jessica, laying a hand on her shoulder, and slid the knife through the duct tape holding her

hands, then her feet. She pulled her right arm forward
and cradled it close.

Sean slipped around to the front and reached for her,
pulling her near, her right arm between them, her left eas-
ing around his neck. In this moment, he didn't think he'd
ever get her close enough. He didn't care who was watching, didn't care what anyone had to say. He just wrapped
her tight and held on, determined to never let her go.

Jessica pulled the blanket up higher with her left hand,
careful to keep her right cradled close in its sling. Her
head pounded in rhythm with her heart rate, the spot
where Joel Mina had driven her into the floor drawing
all of her senses into it. It was that same bump that made
the doctor decide to keep her until morning to ensure her
brain didn't explode.

Outside her door, two nurses padded by, glancing at
her as they moved on.

But inside it was silent except for the throbbing in
her head, a rhythm she wished she could get away from.

Tate had dropped by a few minutes before to pass on
the good news. Joel Mina wasn't saying a word, but Kyle
Randall had started talking the minute Sean delivered
the news of Mina's capture. Jessica's unit was the only
one successfully infiltrated thus far. The remaining men
and women in the photos from Channing's email were
camped in various places around the country, waiting
to take their positions. Homeland was rounding them up
even as Jessica rested uncomfortably in her hospital bed.

Tate had stepped out to see if she was cleared for
something to eat. She wasn't hungry, but it had been an
excuse to get him to leave her by herself for a moment.

Jessica was grateful for his visit, and for Major White's
before him. But the man she really wanted to see had yet

to show his face. Sean had stepped aside when the paramedics appeared, and he'd been gone ever since, having never said another word to her. The way he'd looked at her, something new and different in his expression, had kindled her hope, but it was rapidly burning out. The likelihood that he was already on the way to parts unknown, that he'd left without a goodbye now that the mission was over hung heavy, driving a pain into her chest that rivaled the one in her head.

"Jessica." The voice, hesitant from the door, ramped up her heart rate.

Her pulse fell back and pitched up again as she recognized her father. "Dad?"

His smile was one she hadn't seen before. He stepped into the room and gestured at the chair by her bed, waiting for her permission. When she nodded, he sat down, tossing his jacket onto the foot of the bed. "You look like you failed combatives training."

Jessica swallowed the bitterness. Of course *failure* would be one of his first words to her. But the fact was, it didn't matter anymore. She was her own woman, her own soldier, and she didn't need him to approve of her. Hearing Joel Mina's blind devotion to his father's desires had cured her of that. "You should see the other guy."

He cracked a smile. "So your friend outside tells me." He reached for her hand, his fingers warm on hers. "You did a good thing today. Word has it you probably saved our military. That's pretty powerful stuff."

Her eyes widened. Was that approval? Tears choked her and tried to leak out, but she blinked them back. She might not need him to endorse her decisions, but the fact that he had was a whole new thing.

She cleared her throat. "And you can never tell anyone the awesome thing your daughter did. It has to stay classified." If word ever got out, Mina wouldn't have to deploy his faux army to spread panic. It would happen strictly by word of mouth and his goal would be accomplished for him.

"I know." He squeezed her fingers. "But I don't need that to be proud of you. Fact is, Jessica, I am proud. I just don't always show it. I guess…" He dropped his gaze to their linked hands. "It's a different thing when your daughter goes off to war than when your son does. I've been chest-puffing proud of you, but… A daddy looks at his daughter different, and I guess I thought if I didn't approve, you'd take another career path and be safe. A medic." He shook his head. "There's no more dangerous job on the battlefield, and you proved it throwing yourself in to save your soldiers. I saw the commendation you turned down." His eyes met hers, dry but sad. "I never wanted to lose you but, here we go. I almost did on home soil."

She shook her head, not trusting her voice. He was proud of her? "Dad, I'm not going to become an officer. I'm not going to college. And I'm staying in the Army as a medic."

"As you should."

A knock on the door broke the moment between them, and the nurse stepped in. "Need to check on the patient, if you'd care to wait in the hall?"

Her father stood and pressed a kiss to her forehead. "I hear you're pretty good at patching up soldiers. But forgive the old man if he says a few extra prayers for you every night." He squeezed her fingers. "I'll be in the hall. I have to call your mother and reassure her you're in one piece. She's flying in tomorrow to help you make a late Thanksgiving dinner. Couldn't stomach a ride here from

Virginia on a chopper." He winked and stepped out, a different man than Jessica had ever seen.

The nurse took her vitals, offered more pain meds and was gone before Jessica could put everything together, her head still spinning with her father's confession. She closed her eyes, half wanting to sleep, half afraid she'd wake up and find she'd dreamed that whole encounter with her father. She barely realized the woman left until another presence entered the room.

"Jess?"

Jessica's eyes flew open. Sean. Her pulse throbbed harder, driving into a hard rhythm. "You're still here?"

"Where else would I be?" He looked amused, and more relaxed than she'd ever seen him as he settled into the chair her father had just vacated.

"I don't know." She picked at the blanket. "Virginia. Another mission."

"Not without saying goodbye."

A sick feeling wavered in her chest. "You're leaving?"

"Eventually." He reached for her hand, hesitated, then picked it up in his. "But not until I take a couple of weeks of leave."

The thrill that ran up her arm from his touch made her glad the doctor hadn't hooked her up to a heart monitor. Half the hospital would think she'd coded. "Where are you planning on taking that leave?"

His fingers entwined with hers, his thumb running a hypnotizing rhythm up the side of her hand, sending flutters into her stomach. "Here? I heard somebody needed her shutters painted."

Jessica choked on a laugh. "But not her grass mowed. That's been done."

He chuckled with her, then grew quieter, his hand stilling in hers as he caught her eye. "I'm serious about hanging around for a bit. I want time with you without terrorists chasing our every move. If that's something you'd be interested in."

Jessica nodded slowly, afraid to speak or she'd tell him what was truly on her mind—that she was already in love with him.

"The major said I can stay with him. Keep everything above board, you know."

"I know." She held back a smile that would tinge her swollen lip with pain.

"I need to warn you, though." A smile quirked the side of Sean's lip. "I think it's pretty possible I'll be around longer than two weeks. If that's okay with you."

"It's more than okay."

"Because, you know, I promised you gravy."

She laughed again, this time through tears that refused to be held back.

Sean swallowed hard. "I'm pretty sure, Jessica Dylan, that I'm crazy in love with you."

"Back at you." Her voice was a hoarse whisper.

Sean finally smiled fully, his grin bigger than she'd ever seen it. He leaned forward and pressed a kiss to the side of her mouth, a kiss that promised more than this moment—and more than his heart.

EPILOGUE

Jessica placed a pan of sweet potato casserole on the stove. From the living room, the NBA play-offs blasted through the house, her dad and Major White arguing over which team was going to take down the other. They hadn't moved since they'd settled in after the Easter service.

It was all way too domestic. Just like the discussion she was having with Sean. "I'm telling you. Turkey for Thanksgiving. Ham for Easter."

"So what's Christmas?" He leaned against the counter and crossed his arms.

Jessica swiped hair off her forehead with her wrist, and Sean reached over to tuck the loose tendril behind her ear. She almost shivered at his touch. Five months since he'd first kissed her, five months since he'd started spending every spare moment of leave he could at the major's house, five months—and she still couldn't get enough. She shook off the emotion before she kissed him right here in her own kitchen over the mashed potatoes with her mother looking on. "Christmas is both."

Sean cast a heated glance at her lips as if he knew what she was thinking, then turned to her mother at the sink. "You have rules for holiday food?"

Her mother nodded, swiping the dishrag over a small bowl. "You could say that. It's more habit than law. And what was your food tradition?"

"Venison." Sean sliced the air with his hand. "All the time."

Venison. Jessica had yet to like the game, no matter how Sean had cooked it. She couldn't get over the childhood thought she was eating Bambi's mother.

Jessica's own mother pulled the stopper from the sink. "Well, I'm going to let you two duke it out. I'm going into the living room to see if I can find something besides sports for the men to watch."

"Not an easy task," Sean called to her retreating form. She was barely out of the room before he reached out and grabbed Jessica by the waist, pulling her close to him as he leaned back against the counter. His arms locked behind her waist, trapping her hands at his chest. "I saw that look you gave me a while ago."

"What look?" She refused to give in that easily, even though she definitely wanted to.

"The one that said you were going to kiss me whether your mom was watching or not."

"You were mistaken, sir." If she didn't stop staring at his lips, he'd know she was lying.

"Oh?" His eyebrow arched over blue eyes sparking with things Jessica couldn't even begin to handle. "So what would it take for you to kiss me?"

"For you to never make me eat Bambi meat again."

He threw his head back and laughed. "Can't promise you that."

She sighed. "Fine."

He tilted his head back down, gaze capturing hers. "What if I told you I'm getting out of the Army so I can follow you wherever the military sends you?"

All humor evaporated from the moment. Jessica tried to step back, but he held her tight. "What?" Sean couldn't leave the Army for her. It was his life. He'd resent her. They'd never even so much as discussed it.

"I'm thinking it's time for me to step away from guns and missions. Time to go back to my first love."

Sean had confessed the nightmares still crept up on him at times, worse after he'd taken on a mission with Ethan to find the hacker who'd wreaked havoc on his team. When the trail went cold, Tate took over the search while Sean stepped back. With distance, the visions had dialed back, but Sean still fought them on occasion. He'd said more than once he needed time to heal.

He cleared his throat. "I finally talked to one of the docs and he agreed a change of scenery might be good for me. So I'm getting out. Going to join Ashley's company and take down the bad guys from behind my computer like I always wanted."

Jessica grinned. He was right about going after his first love. She'd watched him many nights devising code, new ways to tear down terrorists at their source. "Sounds good."

"You missed the best part, though." He pressed his forehead against hers.

"What's that?"

His voice lowered. "So I can follow you wherever the military sends you."

Jessica's heart nearly stopped beating. "Are you…?"

He pulled a hand from behind her back and held it up between them, a diamond flickering on the tip of his ring finger. "Will you let me do that? Tag along around the world with you? Send you care packages when you deploy? Meet you at the airport when you come home for R & R?" He wagged his eyebrows at her, then eased closer, letting his lips hover against hers. "Say yes," he whispered.

Jessica didn't say anything. Just closed the gap between them and gave him her answer with a kiss she never wanted to end. A kiss that promised him the rest of her life, whether under the same roof or on opposite sides of the world.

A kiss that promised him forever.

* * * * *

Dear Reader,

You have no idea how grateful I am for you! I'm also grateful to Leslie Herlick, for being all stealthy and adding realism to the scenes at the Soldier Center; to Ben Cash, who might be a mad awesome meteorologist in the real world but who is a seriously scary suspense scene brainstormer at heart; and to my daughter, who likes to write alongside me. And, as always, to my husband, who answers the world's dumbest Army questions with massive amounts of love and patience.

I am so glad you took the time to get to know Sean and Jessica, and I hope you enjoyed the visits from Ethan and Ashley, as well. While Sean's war experience was extreme, our soldiers fight battles every day. Battles that they can never fully describe, even to their families. They bear scars, some seen and some unseen. No soldier returns from war unchanged. No family welcomes their warrior home to the same environment they left behind. The beautiful thing is that, in most cases, life moves forward with new joys and new experiences.

Sometimes, though, the unseen wounds fester and fell even the strongest of soldiers.

On September 11, 2001, I had to tell my second period freshman civics class that the whole world had changed forever. Like all of us who remember that day, the image and emotion is still vivid. In that room I taught two brothers, Jon and Aaron, who wanted nothing more than to serve their country. When 9/11 happened, you could see the resolve solidify. Both joined the Army. Both served overseas in the War on Terror. Both came home.

But only one survived.

I was standing in front of my third-period writing

class in September 2011 when I received another life-altering message. Aaron was gone. The kid whose sarcastic humor and mischievous smile got the best of this teacher on more than one occasion had become a casualty of the war that followed him home. On home turf, alone, Aaron left us to wonder how he could survive a war and yet have the pain steal him away.

Post-traumatic stress disorder is as real and painful a wound as any physical trauma, one our nation is only just now beginning to realize. It is not weakness. It is not shameful. It is an internal injury in need of treatment.

Join me in praying for our men and women who fight the good fight on our behalf. Pray for their families, as well. Visit www.ptsd.va.gov to learn more. And thank a service member. Believe it or not, those expressions of gratitude mean the world to them and the ones who love them.

Also, I'd love to hear from you. You can visit me at www.jodiebailey.com or email me at jodie@jodiebailey.com. I'd love to chat.

Until next time…
Jodie Bailey

COMING NEXT MONTH FROM
Love Inspired® Suspense

Available February 2, 2016

RANSOM • *Northern Border Patrol*
by Terri Reed
When Liz Cantrell's sister is kidnapped and a necklace is demanded as ransom, the antiques dealer must work with agent Blake Fallon to bring down a jewel smuggling ring—and keep her sister alive.

PLAIN DANGER • *Military Investigations*
by Debby Giusti
Speechwriter Carrie York never expected inheriting her father's estate near Amish country would put her in peril. But someone is targeting her, and now she must depend on Tyler Zimmerman—her military policeman neighbor—to survive.

NAVY SEAL SECURITY • *Men of Valor*
by Liz Johnson
Wounded navy SEAL Luke Dunham's top priority is returning to active duty—until he meets physical therapist Mandy Berg. A ruthless stalker is after Mandy, and Luke will risk anything to save her...even his career.

ROCKY MOUNTAIN PURSUIT • by Mary Alford
Presumed dead, agent Jase Bradford thought he'd left the CIA behind. But when Reyna Peterson, his former colleague's widow, shows up at his mountain hideaway with dangerous men on her tail, he can't turn away a woman in trouble.

INTERRUPTED LULLABY • by Dana R. Lynn
Police lieutenant Dan Willis finally tracks down Maggie Slade, who disappeared after her husband's murder months ago, and discovers he isn't the only one who's been searching for the new mother. The killer has found her, as well.

UNDER DURESS • by Meghan Carver
After thugs fail to capture attorney Samantha Callahan and her adopted daughter, her former law school classmate Reid Palmer offers his protection...and his help determining why the criminals are in hot pursuit.

LISCNM0116

REQUEST YOUR FREE BOOKS!
2 FREE RIVETING INSPIRATIONAL NOVELS
PLUS 2 FREE MYSTERY GIFTS

Love Inspired®
SUSPENSE
RIVETING INSPIRATIONAL ROMANCE

YES! Please send me 2 FREE Love Inspired® Suspense novels and my 2 FREE mystery gifts (gifts are worth about $10). After receiving them, if I don't wish to receive any more books, I can return the shipping statement marked "cancel." If I don't cancel, I will receive 4 brand-new novels every month and be billed just $4.99 per book in the U.S. or $5.49 per book in Canada. That's a savings of at least 17% off the cover price. It's quite a bargain! Shipping and handling is just 50¢ per book in the U.S. and 75¢ per book in Canada.* I understand that accepting the 2 free books and gifts places me under no obligation to buy anything. I can always return a shipment and cancel at any time. Even if I never buy another book, the two free books and gifts are mine to keep forever.

123/323 IDN GH5Z

Name _____ (PLEASE PRINT)

Address _____ Apt. #

City _____ State/Prov. _____ Zip/Postal Code

Signature (if under 18, a parent or guardian must sign)

Mail to the **Reader Service:**
IN U.S.A.: P.O. Box 1867, Buffalo, NY 14240-1867
IN CANADA: P.O. Box 609, Fort Erie, Ontario L2A 5X3

Are you a current subscriber to Love Inspired® Suspense books
and want to receive the larger-print edition?
Call 1-800-873-8635 or visit www.ReaderService.com.

* Terms and prices subject to change without notice. Prices do not include applicable taxes. Sales tax applicable in N.Y. Canadian residents will be charged applicable taxes. Offer not valid in Quebec. This offer is limited to one order per household. Not valid for current subscribers to Love Inspired Suspense books. All orders subject to credit approval. Credit or debit balances in a customer's account(s) may be offset by any other outstanding balance owed by or to the customer. Please allow 4 to 6 weeks for delivery. Offer available while quantities last.

Your Privacy—The Reader Service is committed to protecting your privacy. Our Privacy Policy is available online at www.ReaderService.com or upon request from the Reader Service.
We make a portion of our mailing list available to reputable third parties that offer products we believe may interest you. If you prefer that we not exchange your name with third parties, or if you wish to clarify or modify your communication preferences, please visit us at www.ReaderService.com/consumerschoice or write to us at Reader Service Preference Service, P.O. Box 9062, Buffalo, NY 14240-9062. Include your complete name and address.

LIS15

*Inheriting her estranged father's house near
Amish country puts this speechwriter in grave danger.*

*Read on for a sneak preview of
PLAIN DANGER by* Debby Giusti.

Bailey's plaintive howl snapped Carrie York awake with a start. The Irish setter had whined at the door earlier. After letting him out, she must have fallen back to sleep.

Raking her hand through her hair, Carrie rose from the bed and peered out the window into the night. Streams of moonlight cascaded over the field behind her father's house and draped the freestanding kitchen house, barn and chicken coop in shadows. In the distance, she spotted the dog, seemingly agitated as he sniffed at something hidden in the tall grass.

"Hush," she moaned as his wail continued. The neighbors on each side of her father's property—one Amish, the other a military guy from nearby Fort Rickman—wouldn't appreciate having their slumber disturbed by a rambunctious pup who was too inquisitive for his own good.

Still groggy with sleep, she pulled on her clothes, stumbled into the kitchen and flicked on the overhead light. Her coat hung on a hook in the anteroom. Slipping it on, she opened the back door and stepped into the cold night.

"Bailey, come here, boy."

Again the dog's cry cut through the night.

The dog sniffed at something that lay at his feet. A dead animal perhaps? Maybe a deer?

"Bailey, come."

The dog glanced at her, then turned back to the downed prey.

A stiff breeze blew across the field. She shivered and wrapped the coat tightly around her neck, feeling vulnerable and exposed, as if someone were watching… and waiting.

Letting out a deep breath to ease her anxiety, she slapped her leg and called to the dog. "Come, boy. We need to go inside."

Reluctantly, Bailey trotted back to where she stood.

"Good dog." She patted his head and scratched under his neck. Feeling his wet fur, she raised her hand and stared at the tacky substance that darkened her fingers.

She gasped. Even with the lack of adequate light, the stain looked like blood.

"Are you hurt?"

The dog barked twice.

Bending down, she wiped her hand on the dew-damp grass, then stepped closer to inspect the carcass of the fallen animal.

Holding her breath to ward off the cloying odor, she stared down at the pile of fabric.

Her heart pounded in her chest. A deafening roar sounded in her ears. She whimpered, wanting to run. Instead she held her gaze.

Not a deer.

But a man.

Don't miss PLAIN DANGER by Debby Giusti,
available February 2016 wherever
Love Inspired® Suspense books and ebooks are sold.